THE GIRLS OF CANBY HALL®

WHAT'S A GIRL TO DO?

EMILY CHASE

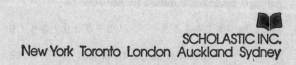

SCHOLASTIC INC.
New York Toronto London Auckland Sydney

ISBN 9-590-33707-6

12 11 10 9 8 7 6 5 4 3   5 6 7 8 9 / 8 0 / 9

Printed in the U. S. A.   06

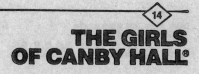

THE GIRLS
OF CANBY HALL®

WHAT'S A
GIRL TO DO?

THE GIRLS
OF CANBY HALL®

Roommates
Our Roommate is Missing
You're No Friend of Mine
Keeping Secrets
Summer Blues
Best Friends Forever
Four is a Crowd
The Big Crush
Boy Trouble
Make Me a Star
With Friends Like That . . .
Who's The New Girl?
Here Come the Boys
What's a Girl to Do?

CHAPTER ONE

"Faith Thompson, are you crazy or what?" The voice belonged to Casey Flint, peeking out from behind the open door of Baker House.

Faith came running up the steps to the dormitory and didn't break stride as she rushed inside.

"It's got to be at least twenty below out there," Casey exaggerated, "and you're jogging! In boots yet," she added, shaking her head. "When did you start running?"

"I wasn't jogging," Faith replied with a shiver in her voice. She unbuttoned her parka and showed Casey her camera, then carefully lifted the strap over her head. "Hold this while I try to peel my frozen coat off of me."

Casey accepted the camera and almost dropped it. "This thing feels like an ice cube. How long were you out there?"

"About an hour," Faith admitted. "I was taking pictures for the *Clarion*," she ex-

1

plained. Faith was the school paper's star photographer, and took her job seriously. She had to, if she was going to reach the ten year goal she had set for herself. It was Faith's secret ambition to become a top news photographer by the time she was twenty-five.

"You were taking pictures for an assignment?" Casey asked.

"Sort of," Faith hedged. She hung up her coat on one of the wooden hooks and turned back to Casey. "I was looking for some hidden signs of spring," she admitted with a grin.

"You're kidding," Casey snorted. "I've got a better idea. Take your boots off and snap some shots of the hidden signs of frostbite," she giggled.

Faith nodded and sat down on the bottom step to pull her boots off.

"You've got to be one dedicated photographer to get up so early on a Sunday morning and brave this weather," Casey concluded. "Dedicated — or crazy."

"Probably both," Faith replied. "I think I got some good shots though, so it was worth it."

"All your pictures are good," Casey complimented. "That's why you're the best photographer the school newspaper's ever had."

"Thank you," Faith answered. "What are you doing up so early?" she asked.

"Sign ups," Casey explained. She placed the camera on the hall table and walked over to help Faith with her boots.

"What sign ups?" Faith asked.

Casey was straddling Faith's leg and quickly glanced back over her shoulder to see if Faith was teasing her. "Kimble's sign up sheets for his social studies project," she explained. "Don't you remember? We either sign up to do some community involvement project for six weeks or take the final exam. The sheets are posted over at the administration building this morning. It's first come, first serve," Casey added, pulling on the boot again. "This boot is cemented on," she grunted. Yet even as she said it, the boot came off, propelling Casey half way across the hall.

"What time is it now?" Faith asked, trying not to laugh.

Casey staggered to her feet and eyed the second boot with a very determined glint in her eyes. Faith promptly grabbed the banister again and giggled.

"Almost nine now," Casey announced as she attacked the second boot with real gusto. "I'm waiting for Keith," she panted between pulls. The boot came off and Casey stood up with a sigh. "Keith and I decided to sign up for the same project so we could work together. It was all his idea." She gave Faith a silly grin, and that said it all.

It was a fact that Casey Flint was crazy about Keith Milford. All the girls knew it, but no one dared tease Casey about it. Keith and two other boys, Sheffield Adams and Terry O'Shaughnessy, lived in the basement of Baker House. They shared an apartment right next to the laundry room. The boys were part of an experiment. They were the first boys to attend Canby Hall. Since its inception, Canby Hall had always been an all girls' boarding school. Then, last quarter, Patrice Allardyce, the school's ultraconservative headmistress, broke tradition. She announced to the stunned girls that the campus might become coed! It was just a possibility, Miss Allardyce had cautioned, and the three boys now in residence would determine if the transition would work. If all went well, and the change was smooth, then more boys would be included the following semester.

"Do you know what project you're going to sign up for?" Casey asked Faith.

"Not really," Faith admitted. She realized she was still wearing her ski cap and took it off, patting her curly afro as she thought about Casey's question. "Dana and Shelley thought it would be a good idea if we all signed up for the same project," she explained. "So we could get each other out of bed, but we haven't really talked about what we'd like to do. The only time the three of us can work is Saturday mornings. I don't know, Casey," Faith added. "Maybe my roommates and I should just forget the project and take the exam."

"Girl, you are crazy! Mr. Kimble's social studies class is the toughest! If you three don't sign up for one of his pet projects, you'll be the only ones. He'll get you for that, trust me," she added with emphasis. "Mr. Kimble prides himself on the fact that *all* his students participate."

"But he gave us a choice," Faith pointed out. "He did say that we could either do the volunteer work and write a short paper about it, *or* take his final exam."

"Faith, have you never wondered why all the kids refer to the test as Kimble's killer exam? For that matter, have you ever met anyone who's taken it . . . and survived?" she asked earnestly.

"Well, I've heard it's tough. . . ."

"Tough? We're talking unbelievable. Look Faith, we're not dealing with a democracy here. You either do the volunteer work or change schools."

"That bad?"

"Remember Mary Lou Becker? She took the exam a couple of years ago."

"Never heard of her," Faith answered.

"I rest my case," Casey said with a nod.

Faith couldn't help laughing. "Okay, you win. I believe you," she said. "I better get moving and wake up Shelley and Dana so we can get over there and sign up."

Casey tossed Faith the boots. "The early bird gets the worm," Casey said with a grin.

"This early worm is going to get pillows thrown in her face when she turns on the light and wakes her roommates up," Faith predicted. She gathered up her possessions and started up the steps. "Duty calls!"

"They'll thank you in the end," Casey called out, her voice melodramatic. The effect was ruined by her laughter.

By the time Faith reached the door to 407, her arms ached from clutching the gloves, scarf, hat and camera, and Dana's boots. She juggled everything around so she could open the door. Reaching for the light switch was impossible so she walked into the darkness and cautiously made her way over to her bed. Without making a sound, she placed everything on the bedspread and then reached for the window blind. Taking a deep breath, she pulled the blind up.

Sunlight poured into the room, casting harsh light against the black walls of the bedroom. In a moment of creative madness, the three roommates had painted the entire bedroom black, from floor to ceiling. The room looked pretty dramatic, with the variety of colorful posters decorating the walls, but with the blinds closed, one was never sure if it was day or night.

The reaction to the light was instantaneous. Dana, her long brown hair partially covering her face, flipped over from front to back in one fluid motion, and pulled the covers up over her head. She didn't make a sound.

Shelley wasn't as quiet. She bolted upright, pushed the curly blonde hair out of her face and squinted at Faith. "What time is it?" she gasped. "If I miss French class again. . . ."

"Relax, Shelley," Faith said, grinning. "It's Sunday."

"Sunday!" Panic left Shelley's face. She groaned with relief and threw herself back down on the bed, covering her eyes with her pillow while she muttered several remarks about her roommate's warped sense of humor.

Faith heard her and started laughing. "Time to get up," she called out in a cheerful voice. "A whole new day awaits you," she added in a louder voice.

The pillows started flying. Faith dodged them like a pro, and when both Shelley and Dana were sitting up in bed and no longer looked like they were going to attack her, Faith sat down on her bed.

"Is everyone awake?" she asked.

Dana and Shelley exchanged a look of total exasperation.

"I didn't get to sleep until after midnight," Dana yawned.

"Same here," Shelley added. "This better be good, Faith."

"It is," Faith announced. "Today's the day we all sign up for our assignments for Mr. Kimble's social studies class. And if we don't hurry, all the good projects will be taken."

Her announcement was met with groans. "I forgot," Shelley admitted.

"I forgot, too," Faith said. "Casey reminded me. So let's get moving."

"Easier said than done," Shelley replied. "My legs are still asleep."

Dana yawned and stood up. "Have we decided what we're going to sign up for?" she asked as she put her navy blue robe on.

"We don't know what's available," Faith reminded her.

"Right." Dana headed for the door. "Give me ten minutes and I'll be ready," she said. "A quick shower and I'll be as good as new."

Ten minutes turned into thirty, but with Faith's prodding and pushing, the three were finally headed over to Main Building.

They ran into Casey and Keith who were headed back to Baker House.

"We've got some good news and some bad news," Casey announced.

"The sign up sheets aren't posted yet?" Shelley asked.

"Oh, they're up," Keith answered. He was wearing a serious expression and a coat at least three sizes too big for him. But then, that was Keith. He always looked serious, his intense brown eyes magnified by thick horn rimmed glasses, and he always seemed to wear clothes that were either too large or too small for him. He was an inch or two shorter than Casey, but she didn't mind. When she first started dating Keith, she tended to slump whenever they stood next to each other. But that was in the past, when Casey was feeling insecure about her relationship with Keith. Now she stood tall and proud, and held on to Keith's hand for all the world to see. "And that's the good news," Keith continued. "The bad news is that he posted them yesterday afternoon, and almost all of the slots are filled."

"We better get moving," Dana announced.

The three roommates sprinted the rest of the distance. When they reached the bulletin board just inside of Main Building, they studied the sheets without a word.

"Looks like a toss up between helping the local vet or doing hospital work," Shelley said. "There are four openings left with the vet and five left with the hospital. What do you two want to do?"

"I don't know," Dana said. "Shelley, you'd be right at home working with a vet."

"That's true," Faith added with a nod.

"Just because I live in Iowa doesn't mean I'm a pro with animals," Shelley answered. Of the three roommates, Shelley was the only one from a small town.

"Next to this New Yorker, I'd say you were a pro," Dana said.

"We don't see many cows in Washington, D.C. either," Faith said.

"Have either of you ever worked in a hospital?" Shelley asked.

Both Dana and Faith shook their heads. "Then I think we should sign up for Greenleaf Memorial Hospital and all do something we aren't familiar with. Besides," she added, "I've always wanted to work in a hospital. Comes from watching too many soap operas I guess."

"If you're sure," Faith said. She pulled a pen from her pocket, looked at each roommate, and then signed her name. Both Dana and Shelley signed their names after Faith.

They all noted the time on the schedule.

"Okay, we're all set," Dana said. "Eight until twelve every Saturday morning for the next six weeks."

"Right," Faith said. "We'll all set our own alarm clocks so at least one of us gets up."

"You know this could turn out to be kind of fun," Shelley said with real enthusiasm.

"We'll have to get up at six, get dressed, and then walk into Greenleaf, no matter how horrible the weather is," Dana said. "I'm not too sure if that's going to be fun or not."

"Six! We have to get up at six? Hey, wait a minute. Maybe we should rethink this thing. I mean, maybe we should think about taking the exam," Shelley stammered.

"Ever heard of Mary Lou Becker?" Faith asked with a sly smile.

"No," Dana answered. "Why?"

"Oh, never mind," Faith replied. "Come on. Let's jog over to the dining hall and grab some breakfast."

"I hope they have some sweet rolls left," Shelley said as they started out the door.

"Give me some cream cheese and bagels for breakfast, lunch, and dinner and I'd be content," Dana sighed. She was thinking about Sunday mornings at home, and how she and her thirteen-year-old sister, Maggie, would fix a tray full of cream cheese and bagels and hot mugs of tea, and sit Indian style on their mother's bed to share a late morning breakfast. Dana's mother had a high-powered job as a fashion buyer for one of New York City's exclusive stores, and Sunday was just about the only day of the week she could sleep in. The three Morrisons were especially close, more so since Dana's father, John, had remarried after his divorce from Dana's mother.

As close as Dana was to Shelley, she didn't think her roommate really understood how she felt about her divorced parents. Shelley's family was what Dana thought of as the "All American" family. Her parents were happily married and very much in love.

On the other hand, Faith would probably know just how Dana felt. She, too, had lost her father, but in a different, much more terrible way. Faith's father was a dedicated police officer who had been killed when he tried to stop a robbery.

Faith glanced over at Dana and saw that she was frowning, and wondered what she was thinking. Faith wondered, but didn't ask. She respected Dana's privacy, and Shelley's too. Of the three roommates, Faith considered herself the most practical-minded, and the least excitable. She was usually the level-headed one of the group and kept most of her feelings inside. Faith decided her even disposition was the result of being the middle child. She had an older sister, Sarah, and a younger brother, Richard. Faith's mother was a social worker and very dedicated.

"Tryouts for the spring play are coming up, and I have a good chance at the lead,"

Shelley said, breaking the silence. "Tom is going to try out for the male lead. Did I tell you that?"

"About five times," Dana said. She was teasing but couldn't help being a little worried about Shelley. Shelley seemed convinced that the lead was hers.

"Look, Shelley," Faith cautioned, "give it your best shot, but don't get your hopes way up there . . . just in case. . . ."

"Don't worry, Faith," Shelley replied. "I've really checked out the competition and I'm just positive I'll get the lead."

CHAPTER TWO

Dana's mother called from New York City on Sunday evening. It was just a few minutes before study hours started, so the long distance visit was short.

"I'm fine, Mom," Dana said. "I'll write a long letter tomorrow. I promise. How are things with you?"

"Just fine, honey. It's been hectic at work but I'll survive. Maggie and I are disgusted with this weather."

They talked for a few more minutes and then Dana's mother said, "I've pretty much decided that Maggie will be coming to Canby Hall next year. She doesn't say much but I think she's very excited about it."

"Maggie coming to Canby?" Dana stammered. The news was shocking to Dana. She had never considered that her little sister might follow in her footsteps. But it was logical, after all. Dana couldn't understand why she felt so upset.

"Won't that be nice?" her mother continued. Dana could hear the smile in her mother's voice and knew she should feel pleased. She didn't though. "I'll have both of my girls at the same school. And Maggie should have an easy time adjusting, with you there showing her the ropes."

"It's all decided?" Dana whispered the question. She was too stunned to keep her voice steady.

"Well, it's a distinct possibility," her mother qualified. "Look, honey. I better hang up now. Take care of yourself and write. We miss you."

"Right, Mom," Dana replied. "I miss you, too."

Dana hung up but continued to stand in front of the phone, her hand resting on the receiver as she considered all the ramifications of her mother's news. Maggie might be coming to Canby Hall! Dana knew she should be smiling, but found that she couldn't. Inside, she felt like screaming! A knot formed in her stomach, and Dana was honest enough to admit the reason. Guilt. She didn't want her little sister at Canby Hall. Not this year, or the next, she thought. *I've got to think this through*, she told herself.

"Hey, Dana, you through with the phone?"

The intrusion jarred Dana. She let go of the phone and turned to face another Baker House resident, Pamela Young.

"What's with you?" Pamela demanded. "You look like you're going to be sick."

"Thanks," Dana muttered. She moved out of the way so that Pamela could use the phone.

"Bad news?" Pamela asked, a vinegar smile indicating to Dana that she would have been quite pleased if Dana had admitted that she had received bad news. Pamela and Dana were not friends. In fact, Pamela didn't seem to have any friends at all. She was, in Faith's words, a rich brat, the pampered daughter of a famous movie actress. Pamela had money all right, but no manners. Worse, she was terribly self-centered, and really enjoyed causing trouble for people. Dana didn't think Pamela was capable of friendship.

"See you later," Dana mumbled. Before Pamela could reply, Dana turned and raced back to her room. She didn't have time to fence barbs from Pamela. She had some heavy duty thinking to do.

Shelley and Faith were both at their desks, studying. Dana came into the room without saying a word, grabbed her Spanish textbook, and threw herself down on her bed. She turned and faced the wall, a silent message to Shelley and Faith that she wanted to be left alone.

Shelley gave Faith a puzzled look and then asked, "Dana? Who was on the phone? Anyone I know?"

"My mom," Dana answered, her voice a monotone.

"Everything okay?" Shelley persisted, staring at Dana's back. She wasn't just being curious but knew from the way Dana was acting that something was wrong. Shelley was close to both of her roommates, and wanted to help Dana if she could.

Dana glanced over her shoulder and smiled at Shelley. "Everything is fine," she said, trying to sound cheerful and convincing. "Really."

"Right," Faith said. "When you're ready to talk about it, we'll be here." Dana obviously was upset about something and needed time to sort her feelings out.

Shelley decided that she would have to be patient and wait until Dana was ready to share her problem. She opened her book and tried to concentrate on her French assignment but her heart wasn't in it. She found herself daydreaming about the play tryouts. She could just picture herself, standing on the stage right next to Tom. Tom would hand Shelley a dozen red roses in appreciation for her magnificent performance as the leading lady in . . . oh, she hoped it was a play she really liked! Romeo and Juliet would be nice, she considered. She thought she would make a wonderful Juliet and there was no question that Tom would be a fantastic Romeo. Shelley sighed, impatient because she wouldn't find out the name of the play until next Tuesday.

Of the three roommates, Shelley realized that she was the most impatient, and the most emotional. She didn't think those two traits were imperfections, however, but considered them necessary attributes of a budding actress. Tom had once told her that he could always read her mood, just by looking at her face.

Dana stared at her opened book but the words blurred as she thought about her problem. And it was a problem, she admitted to herself. She didn't want her little sister to come to Canby Hall. Yet when she tried to understand why she felt this way, she had no answer. Maggie was a great sister, always laughing and so easygoing. And Maggie would be crushed if she had any idea that Dana felt this way. That thought made Dana feel worse than just guilty. It made her feel ashamed.

She could feel Shelley staring at her, and she knew both her roommates were curious about her silent behavior, but she couldn't talk about Maggie just yet. They would ask her why the thought of Maggie coming to Canby Hall upset her, and Dana couldn't answer. She suddenly shut her book and stood up. "I'm going to bed early tonight," she announced to Shelley and Faith. Before either roommate could question her, Dana grabbed her robe and gown, found a clean towel, and headed for the showers.

As soon as the door shut behind her, Shelley dropped her book and stood up. "What do you think happened?" she asked Faith.

"I don't know," Faith admitted, frowning. "But she'll tell us when she's ready."

"You know, Faith," Shelley said, "I was

just thinking. Both you and Dana are so good at keeping your feelings inside. I don't know how you two do it. I wish I could," she added. "The only reason we know that Dana is upset is because she's being quiet. A stranger wouldn't have the faintest clue anything was wrong."

"I'm not so sure that keeping your feelings inside is such a good idea," Faith told Shelley. "Sometimes problems can settle in your stomach and eat you up inside. Do you know what I mean?"

Shelley shook her head. "Not really. As soon as something happens to me, good or bad, I let everyone know how upset or happy I am. I can't seem to help myself."

"And that's exactly why you'll make a wonderful actress," Faith said. "You know how to express yourself."

"You really think so? That I'll make a good actress I mean?" Shelley asked, unable to keep the eagerness out of her voice. She dearly loved compliments.

"Of course," Faith said, smiling at Shelley's enthusiasm.

Suddenly Shelley said, "Do you think it has something to do with her father?"

"What?" Faith asked. Shelley had a habit of switching subjects in midstream, without pausing for air.

"Dana. Maybe her mom told her something about her dad and his new family," she suggested.

"Look, Shelley," Faith sighed, "It's pointless to speculate. And from what I understand, Dana's father is doing just fine. You're just going to have to wait until Dana tells you."

"You're right," Shelley admitted. "The important thing is that when she does tell us what's going on, we'll be here for her."

The slam of several doors echoing throughout the corridor indicated that Study Hours had ended. Faith stood up and stretched. "Since Dana wants to go to bed, let's go say hello to Casey. Find out what's going on."

Shelley nodded and followed Faith out the door. "Casey should work for a newspaper when she finishes school," she giggled. "She always knows what's going on around here before anyone else does."

The door to Casey's room was wide open but Faith knocked anyway and waited until she was invited in. Faith put great store in respecting everyone's privacy.

"Hi, you guys," Casey called out. She was sitting on her bed, Indian style, with a pile of books surrounding her. "Don't just hover. Come on in," she invited.

Both Shelley and Faith smiled. "We came to find out the latest goings on around here," Shelley said.

"What's the word?" Faith demanded. She could tell by the way Casey was grinning that she knew something no one else did.

"Uniforms!" Casey whispered the word and leaned back against the wall, waiting for a reaction.

Faith was the first to respond. "You want to run that by me one more time? Did you say uniforms?"

"You mean like basketball uniforms, soccer uniforms?" Shelley asked.

"Nope," Casey said. "I'm talking school uniforms."

"You're kidding! You mean wear uniforms to school?" Shelley sputtered, her surprise obvious.

"It's just a possibility," Casey warned them. "Some of the parents have requested that the school look into the possibility. Our sweet headmistress aims to please . . . the parents, that is, because they're the ones who pay the tuition. She thinks it's a good idea, too."

"I need some chips," Shelley muttered, "or a candy bar. Shocking news makes me hungry," she explained. "I'm starting my diet tomorrow," she added as an afterthought.

Casey jumped off the bed and rummaged through her foot locker. She produced a large bag of potato chips and handed it to Shelley. Then she lifted the blinds to the window sill and removed three Tabs from the pyramid stacked there.

"Casey, are you sure about this?" Faith asked as she accepted her drink.

Casey didn't answer. She just gave Faith an exasperated look.

"Stupid question," Faith said. "You're never wrong on your information. How do you find out everything?" she asked, knowing full well Casey would never tell her.

"I never reveal my sources," Casey announced with a smile. She settled herself back on the bed and opened her can.

"I think she sits outside of Ms. Allardyce's house, under one of the bushes, and listens day and night," Shelley decided.

"Well, what do you think?" Casey demanded. "Are you for or against?" she persisted.

"I can't imagine wearing uniforms," Shelley replied. "We'll all look like clones."

"Not all of us," Faith said, grinning, referring to the fact that she was black and most of the girls were white.

"It's just a possibility?" Shelley asked.

"That's the word," Casey explained.

"When will we know for sure?" Faith asked. "And what are the uniforms like?"

"I thought you'd never ask," Casey said with a great deal of enthusiasm. "Now the way I understand it Ms. Allardyce is going to pick out three styles, and then," she paused and grinned at the girls, "are you ready for this?"

Faith and Shelley immediately nodded. "Each dormitory house — Baker, Addison, and Charles — will vote on one girl to be the model. That victim . . . I mean that lucky person, will get to wear one of the uniforms for a whole month. Then, at the end of the month, everyone will have decided which of the three uniforms they like the best, and vote."

"So three girls will be wearing three different uniforms every day for an entire month?" Shelley asked.

"You've got it," Casey answered.

"Then it's really a sure thing," Faith said. "One way or another, we will have uniforms."

"Not so," Casey contradicted. "At the end of the month, we will vote on two issues. The first vote will be *if* we want the uniforms or not. For some reason Ms. Allardyce has decided to be democratic. If the majority vote in favor of uniforms, then we vote again on which style we like."

"Seems kind of silly to me," Shelley said. "I think we should vote right away. If the girls don't want uniforms, then that's the end of it. Why go to the bother of looking at three different styles all month long and then voting against having uniforms at all?"

"Because Ms. Allardyce wants us to have time to think about it. If we see the uniforms every single day for a solid month, she thinks we'll make a better decision."

"I don't know if I'm for or against," Faith admitted to the girls.

"Well I'm glad someone is going to model a uniform from our dorm," Casey said, a sparkle in her eyes.

"Why?" Faith asked, puzzled. She knew that look, and immediately sensed that Casey was up to something.

"Because we all get to vote on one person to wear it for a month," she explained, giggling. "I guess from your blank looks that

I'm just more warped than most people, but I think this is a golden opportunity to get back at a certain obnoxious individual."

"Who?" Shelley asked.

"I'll give you a clue. She's the only girl who changes her clothes before and after every class and every meal, and has never worn the same outfit twice," Casey said. "Her mother happens to be a famous actress with more money than my parents, and she is always causing trouble."

"Pamela!" Both Shelley and Faith yelled out the name at the same time.

"That's right," Casey said, "and each of us has gotten burned by her! I say it's time to quit putting up with her behavior. That's why she gets my vote to wear the uniform."

"She'll get my vote, too," Shelley said. "She won't do it though."

"She'll have to," Casey stated with emphasis. "Whoever gets the most votes has to wear the uniform, like it or not."

Shelley and Faith chuckled all the way back to Room 407. The lights were out and they tried to be as quiet as possible as they hunted for their pajamas. They were doing quite well, until Shelley tripped on the corner of her bed and crashed into the wall. She stubbed her toes and let out a yelp of pain.

When the girls had first moved into the room, they had taken their bed frames apart and put them in storage. The mattresses, with bright spreads and covered with a variety of pillows in contrasting colors, looked like modern sofas. The room had a cozy atmosphere, but in the dark, the beds were extremely tricky to get around.

Faith took mercy on Shelley and turned on the small desk lamp. Dana didn't seem to react to the light. She was sleeping on her side, her face turned to the wall.

Shelley rubbed her toes and then found her robe. When Faith saw that she had everything she needed, she turned the light out again and followed Shelley down the hall to the showers.

Fifteen minutes later the two roommates tiptoed back to the room.

"Where have you guys been all evening?" Dana's voice made Shelley jump. Dana sounded wide awake. "You can turn the light on," she said. "I've been awake a long time. Ever since the earthquake."

"That was me crashing into the wall," Shelley admitted. "I'm sorry I woke you up."

"Don't worry about it," Dana said.

Faith turned on the desk lamp and the room was transformed into a cozy, softly lit area. "So tell me, where did you two go?" Dana asked.

"Down to Casey's room," Faith said. She climbed into bed and pulled the covers over her. "You wouldn't believe the latest bit of news she had to tell us." Faith launched into the news about the uniforms. She didn't pause until she had told it all, including the fact that she and Shelley and Casey were all going to vote for Pamela Young to be the model.

Dana clasped her hands together and laughed. "Pamela will have a fit," she predicted with obvious glee. "A well deserved fit I might add."

"Are you for or against uniforms?" Faith asked.

"My initial reaction is against," Dana said.

"Cost-wise, I'm all for it," Faith said. "I think my mom would like it too. Social workers don't make all that much money and uniforms would certainly help with the budget."

"We'll have a month to decide," Shelley said. "And the uniforms might be nice looking."

"Are you guys too tired to talk about something else before you go to sleep?" Dana asked.

Shelley and Faith exchanged a knowing look. Dana was ready to talk.

"No problem," Faith said. "I'm wide awake. What do you want to talk about?"

Dana looked over at Shelley and waited for her answer. Shelley was working lotion into her neck and face but nodded her encouragement.

"Shelley, you're going to slide out of bed if you use much more of that stuff," Dana said.

"I hate dry skin," Shelley answered. "Better to slide out of bed than risk cracks in my hands or feet." She put the lotion aside and pulled out a jar of Vaseline from her drawer.

"Now what are you doing?" Faith couldn't

resist asking. She and Dana watched, mesmerized, as Shelley applied a liberal amount of the Vaseline on her feet.

"My new beauty treatment," Shelley announced. "First you cover your feet with this stuff and then you put on socks. Then you work a big glob of it on each hand."

"And?" Dana asked.

"And you wear gloves to bed." Shelley pulled out a pair of white elbow length gloves and held them up for the girls to see. Dana immediately started laughing while Faith just shook her head.

"It really works," Shelley insisted.

"Where did you get those gloves?" Faith asked, trying not to laugh. Shelley seemed very serious about her latest beauty method and Faith didn't want her to think she thought she was crazy. She did, but she didn't want Shelley to know it.

"Mom sent them to me. You just can't find long white gloves in Greenleaf," she explained.

"No kidding?" Dana said, shaking her head.

"So quit stalling and tell us what's on your mind," Shelley said to Dana.

"Oh," Dana said. She cleared her throat and then said, "I talked to my mom tonight and, well, it's no big deal or anything but she did mention that my sister, Maggie, might be coming to Canby Hall next semester." Dana looked down at her hands while she spoke.

"That's great!" Shelley's voice was full of

enthusiasm. "You must really be excited," she added as she pulled on her gloves.

Faith didn't say anything. She just looked at Dana and waited for her to continue.

"That's just it," Dana said. "I'm not excited. Not at all. To be real honest, I don't think I want Maggie to come to Canby Hall."

"Why in heaven's name not?" Shelley was truly amazed by Dana's statement.

"I don't know," Dana admitted. Her shoulders slumped and she turned to Faith. "So how come I feel this way?" she asked.

"Maybe because it came as such a surprise," Faith suggested. "You need some time to think about it. Besides, you said might," she continued, "and that means it isn't settled, right?"

"Mom said it was just a possibility," Dana answered.

"Well, I think you should be happy," Shelley muttered. "Honestly, Dana, I don't understand why you're not. *I* would be thrilled."

"Shelley, you don't have a sister so you can't possibly know how you'd feel," Faith reminded her. "You might think you'd feel one way or another, but you can't know." Faith couldn't keep the exasperation out of her voice. Sometimes Shelley was quite stubborn in her views.

"Well . . . maybe," Shelley conceded. "So why aren't you excited?" she asked Dana again. "Explain so I'll understand."

Dana shrugged. "I don't know. Maybe Faith is right. It just came as a big surprise.

I'll probably get excited about it when I think some more."

Shelley nodded. "That's the spirit. A good night's sleep and I bet you'll wake up full of enthusiasm," she predicted.

"Right," Dana answered, trying her best to sound cheerful and optimistic. Deep down inside, she really didn't agree with Shelley, but Shelley's reaction depressed her. She felt more guilty now than she did before she told her the news.

What was the matter with her anyway? How could she expect her roommates to understand her reaction to Maggie possibly coming to Canby Hall when she didn't understand it herself?

Perhaps she should pay Alison a visit. Alison was the housemother of Baker House and was really good at listening to problems. Dana thought that was because she was so young, only twenty-six years old, and so she was more in tune with how the girls thought. Alison lived in an apartment in the attic of Baker House, and always welcomed visitors. She was a special person, and a good friend.

Yes, Dana determined, she *would* talk to Alison. But only if the possibility turned to a reality, and Maggie was really going to come to Canby Hall. Then she would have to deal with her feelings, like it or not.

With a sigh of exhaustion, Dana plopped down on the bed and closed her eyes. Things would be better in the morning, wouldn't they?

CHAPTER THREE

It was easy to put the problem of Maggie aside once the school week started. The Monday assembly, with the announcement that uniforms were being considered, caused quite an uproar. All the girls immediately separated into two groups, those for and those against.

By Tuesday evening, the buzz hadn't died down one bit. Faith and Dana were sitting in the cafeteria with their trays of food. Both were listening to bits of conversation from the other tables.

"Boy, everyone is getting involved in this uniform issue," Dana said, shaking her head. "And no one is neutral. They're either all for it, or totally against it."

"One person is neutral," Faith corrected.

"Who?"

"Pamela Young. She didn't go to the assembly and she acts like she could care less."

"Pamela always . . ." Dana dropped her

29

voice to a whisper. "Here comes Pamela now," she said.

"Good evening, Pamela," Faith called out. "Care to join us?" she asked, knowing full well Pamela would never do such a thing. Pamela was very obvious in her dislike for Faith and Dana. In fact, disliking was a full time occupation with Pamela, Faith thought. She disliked just about everyone and everything.

Pamela paused at their table, her tray balanced against the most beautiful teal blue jumpsuit Dana had ever seen. Dana had a keen eye for fashion, inherited from her mother, and knew an original when she saw one. "That jumpsuit must have cost a fortune," she blurted out before she could stop herself.

"Of course it did," Pamela answered in a condescending voice Dana hated. "I'm surprised you recognize quality," she added, giving Dana's outfit a once-over. "I can't join you," she continued, "my friends are waiting for me."

What friends? Faith wanted to ask. Instead, she said, "How do you feel about uniforms? Are you for or against?"

"I couldn't care less," Pamela stated. She sounded quite bored. "I'm not going to vote. It's all so stupid, don't you think?"

Before Faith and Dana could answer, Pamela walked away.

"The princess is definitely going to get my vote," Faith told Dana.

"Princess?"

"That's Casey's nickname for Pamela," Faith explained. "It fits, doesn't it?"

Dana nodded and burst out laughing. "That it does. Oh look, here comes Shelley."

Dana waved and Shelley hurried over to the table with her tray.

"How did drama go?" Faith asked.

"Super," Shelley replied. "The play is going to be great, just great. It's called *Spring Fancy*, and it's a romantic comedy, and Tom is going to be wonderful as the lead and I . . . ."

"Hold it," Dana interrupted, grinning. "Slow down and catch your breath. We'll be here for as long as it takes you to tell us every single detail. We promise."

Shelley smiled and took a deep breath. "I ran all the way over here so I wouldn't miss you guys. I couldn't wait to tell you."

"So tell us," Faith demanded.

"Well, I haven't read much of the play. I only just got it," she explained, "but the first scene is a real knock out. The female lead is named Rachael. Isn't that a beautiful name? Anyway, Tom and I are going to get together and practice before tryouts. I mean, I know I've got the part all sewn up . . . everyone says so, but I still want to give the reading the best I've got."

"When are the tryouts?" Dana asked when Shelley paused for air.

"Next week," Shelley explained. "And oh, Faith, guess what? Rachael sings this fantastic love song at the very beginning of the scene. She's all alone, and she thinks she'll never fall in love and. . . ."

"Hold it," Dana said. "I thought you said it was a romantic comedy. You mean it's a musical too?"

"No, there's just this one song that the heroine sings at the very beginning, that's all."

"You've got to sing?" Faith was trying hard not to laugh. Singing wasn't one of Shelley's pluses. It was, Faith admitted, a definite minus.

"Just the one song," Shelley said with exasperation. "No problem, I can handle it," she predicted with a shrug. "Quit frowning, Faith. Really, it will be easy."

"If you say so," Faith replied, totally unconvinced.

"So it's a good play?" Dana interjected, smiling. When Shelley nodded, Dana continued, "We'll help you get ready, okay?"

"Great," Shelley said. She picked up her fork and looked at her plate. "What *is* this stuff?" she asked.

"I don't know," Faith told her. "It tastes like rubber, though. I think the cook is stealing old tennis shoes and converting them into stew. That green stuff is peas."

"It's not *too* bad," Shelley said after she took a small bite. "Just don't look at it while you eat. That's the secret."

"Shelley, you're impossible," Dana told her. "You'll eat anything."

"I just don't like to waste," Shelley said. "Sure could go for a pizza though. Too bad we can't walk into town and eat at Pizza Pete's."

"It's too dark, and besides, pretty soon we have to vote on the uniforms. I don't want to miss that," Dana said.

"I'm meeting Johnny for pizza tomorrow after school," Faith stated. "If you want, I'll bring you guys a pizza."

"Great," Shelley said. "Tell Johnny hi for me," she added.

Faith smiled and nodded. She and Johnny had met last year, and had been going together ever since. Johnny went to Greenleaf High School and lived with his family in town. He was tall, and extremely handsome, with warm brown eyes that made Faith still find herself holding her breath when he gave her that special look of his.

"Earth to Faith, come in," Dana said.

Faith shook her head and grinned. "Caught me daydreaming," she admitted. "What were you saying?"

"You were thinking about Johnny, weren't you?" Shelley guessed. "I could tell you were, so don't deny it."

"Oh yeah? How could you tell?" Faith asked.

"Easy," Shelley answered. "At least, easy for me. I'm going to be an actress, remember. And actresses have to tune in to all the different expressions. You looked 'dreamy', that's all."

"Hurry up and finish," Dana said. "I want to get some seats in the lounge," she said.

"Why do we need seats?" Faith asked. "We're just going to vote, aren't we?"

"No. First we have to listen to the debate. Nancy Plummer is going to present an argument for uniforms, and Heather is going to argue against. It's going to be fun," she added, "so let's get moving."

The three girls hurried to put their trays on the conveyor belt and literally raced back to Baker House.

They walked into the lounge, their faces a bright red from the cold, and immediately spotted Casey. She was sitting over to the side and motioned to them to join her.

"Too bad Pamela isn't here," Casey told the girls when they were settled next to her. "I've got a feeling she's going to win."

"By win, you mean lose, don't you?" Faith said.

"I don't get it," Shelley said. "How come we have to listen to a debate? We're just voting on who gets to wear the uniform, aren't we?"

"Yes," Dana answered.

"So why the debate?"

"So Nancy and Heather can get some practice in. They're both on the debate team, remember?"

Alison, her hair a reddish brown blur as she raced into the room, clapped her hands together and called for order. "Okay," she announced, "Nancy gets ten minutes to pre-

sent her argument and then Heather gets ten.
Then we vote on the girl who will model one
of the uniforms. Let's all be quiet and listen."

Dana, Faith, Shelley, and Casey all listened
to both sides. Nancy and Heather had really
prepared their arguments well, and Shelley
found herself agreeing with both sides.

Then everyone voted. It was agreed that
Alison would count the votes and Sheffield
Adams, the gorgeous and very sophisticated
black student Faith used to have quite a
crush on, would write down the names and
numbers.

Sheff's job turned out to be extremely easy,
and a little embarrassing for him. All but two
votes were stacked in the same pile, for the
same candidate, Pamela Young. She won by
a landslide, just as Casey had predicted. Only
two people didn't vote for her. They voted
for Sheff.

"Keith and Terry, I'm going to get you for
this," Sheff announced when he saw that he
had received two votes. He was grinning, and
Faith knew he was taking it all in good fun.

"What makes you think we voted for you?"
Terry O'Shaughnessy, a freckle-faced redhead
and a notorious prankster called back. Even
as he spoke, he and Keith were edging out of
the room. Sheff excused himself and bolted
after his two roommates.

"Sheff, you've got great legs," Casey called
after him. "You'll look terrific in a little
pleated skirt."

All the girls laughed, and Sheff paused at

the door, giving Casey one of his raised eyebrow looks. "First I'm going to take care of my roommates, Casey, and then I'm coming after you," he threatened.

"Who's going to tell Pamela she won?" Shelley asked Alison when the laughter died down.

"Casey, why don't you go get Pamela and tell her to come down to the lounge," Alison suggested. "The rest of you girls can go and get started on your homework," she suggested. "Study Hours started ten minutes ago."

There were several protests, but in the end, everyone went back to their rooms to hit the books.

It wasn't until nine, when Study Hours had ended, that Casey came to tell them Pamela's reaction. "She didn't take it well," Casey said with a cat-who-just-caught-the-canary grin. It was obvious to Dana, Shelley, and Faith that Casey was loving every minute of this.

"That bad, huh?" Dana asked, grinning back.

"We're talking totally grim," Casey replied. She sat down on Faith's bed and let out a whoop of laughter. "It was wonderful," she admitted. "Truly wonderful."

"Did she scream and yell?" Shelley asked.

"No," Casey replied. "Pamela said she wouldn't do it, of course, but then Alison came up and told her rules were rules and that she *had* to wear the uniform. Pamela stomped out of the room in a real huff. She threatened to get Alison fired and said she was going to call her mother."

"Has anyone seen these uniforms yet?" Faith asked. "Maybe they aren't so bad."

"Only Ms. Allardyce has seen them," Casey said. "Pamela doesn't have to wear hers until next week."

"I'm going to take a shower," Shelley announced, heading out the door.

"I've got to do a load of laundry," Casey said. "I'll see you guys later. Hey Dana, that's great about your sister coming up here next year."

Before Dana could do more than open her mouth, the door closed behind Casey.

"Now how did she find that out?" Dana asked Faith.

"Shelley probably told her," Faith said. "You didn't tell her it was a secret."

"It's okay that Casey knows," Dana said. "She's a good friend. I just wish that Shelley would understand how I feel, but she doesn't."

"What don't I understand?" Shelley stood at the doorway, wearing a frown and her fuzzy pink robe. "I forgot my toothbrush," she added.

"I was just telling Faith that I didn't think you understand that I really don't want Maggie to come here. That's all."

"Well, you're absolutely right. I don't understand. What's the matter with you?" Shelley shook her head.

"Okay, Shelley, I'll try to explain," Dana

answered. She stood up and started to pace around the room. "I've always been responsible for Maggie in the past. I've had to, you know, watch out for her, take care of her. Up here, I'm on my own, and I like it that way. I have my own friends and my own space. If Maggie comes up here, I'll have to go back to being the big sister full time again. I know I'm being selfish but I can't seem to help it."

"You are being selfish," Shelley said. "Maggie is family. I can't believe you feel this way."

"Shelley, try not to judge," Faith advised. She could sense that Dana was getting good and angry with Shelley and found herself a little irritated, too.

"Canby Hall is mine," Dana said, raising her voice. "Mine! Not Maggie's. Let her find her own school," she said.

"That's ridiculous," Shelley scoffed. "You are being childish and selfish, Dana, and that isn't like you. If I had a sister. . . ."

"Here we go again," Dana muttered, rolling her eyes heavenward.

"Okay you two, knock it off," Faith said. "Shelley, I think you should quit trying to make Dana feel the way *you* think she should feel. And Dana, don't you get upset about this. It's not a reality yet. You might be getting yourself all worked up for nothing. Maggie might not come to Canby Hall, remember?"

Shelley marched into the room, grabbed her toothbrush, and turned around. "Well I still think you're being very childish, Dana, and now that I've had my say, I will *never, ever* bring up the subject again."

She hurried out of the room, followed by Dana's irritated sigh.

"She really doesn't understand," Faith said, in defense of Shelley.

"Do you?" Dana asked, letting the vulnerability show in her voice.

"I'm trying to," Faith answered. "I've got a sister, too, remember. Sarah is older so I haven't had to look out for her like you've looked after Maggie, but I think I know how you're feeling."

"Oh? And how's that?" Dana sat down on the bed and folded her hands. She was feeling better already, just because she was finally admitting to her roommates, and to herself, how she really felt.

"Guilty," Faith answered. She tilted her chair back and propped her feet on her desk. "Am I right?"

"Yes," Dana replied. "Guilty and ashamed. I haven't felt this awful since I broke my arm years ago. Only this time the pain is inside, not outside. You know what I mean?"

Faith nodded.

"So now what do I do?"

"Think about it," Faith suggested. "Give yourself some time. Maybe you'll change your mind. There really isn't anything you can do, is there?"

"No," Dana admitted. "I could tell my mom that I don't want Maggie to come, but

I won't. She would never understand, and it would hurt Maggie too much to know how I really felt," Dana concluded.

"So do what my mom suggests whenever I have a problem I can't solve right away."

"What's that?" Dana asked.

"Don't do anything. Some things just work out all by themselves."

Later that night, when everyone was in bed, and the lights were out, Dana stared into the darkness and thought about Maggie.

"Dana, are you still awake?" Shelley's soft voice floated across the room in the darkness.

"Yes," Dana answered.

"I just wanted to ask you something," Shelley whispered.

"What?"

"Are you mad at me?"

"No, Shelley, I'm not mad."

"Good!"

"Good-night, Shelley."

A few minutes of silence elapsed and then Dana whispered, "Shelley?"

"Yes?"

"You wearing your gloves to bed again?"

"Sure," Shelley answered with a giggle. Dana joined in the soft laughter and then a third voice started laughing.

"I know it looks stupid," Shelley said, "but when my hands are soft and smooth and your hands are all chapped and ugly and cracked . . . ."

Faith and Dana's groans drowned out the rest of Shelley's speech.

CHAPTER FOUR

The next week Shelley was so busy studying her lines for the coming tryouts that the week just seemed to fly by. Before she knew it, it was Friday night, and she was waiting for Tom to pick her up for their date.

She sat at her desk finishing her letter to her boyfriend back home.

"Writing to Paul?" Dana asked from the doorway.

"Just finishing," Shelley said. "Dana, do you think this skirt looks okay?" she asked. She stood up and twirled around. "It feels a little tight around the waist."

"Looks great," Dana told her. "Tom's waiting downstairs," she added.

Shelley smiled with anticipation. She quickly sprinkled some of her favorite perfume on the pink envelope and then sealed it. She and Tom could mail her letter to Paul on their way to the show.

The fact that Shelley had two boyfriends

didn't bother her at all. Tom knew all about Paul, and Paul knew all about Tom. The two boys had met once, when Paul had arrived at Canby Hall for a surprise visit.

The nice thing about having two boyfriends was that Shelley didn't have to choose between them. Paul lived in Pine Bluff, Iowa, and after his visit to Canby Hall had agreed that they should both date other people.

Of course, Tom and Shelley had no such agreement. Shelley couldn't imagine Tom wanting to date anyone else! Why, there wasn't another girl on the entire campus who shared Tom's interests. They were, Shelley considered, perfect for each other!

Dana watched Shelley fly down the corridor. She looked like a fluffy pink something or other, Dana thought, smiling. She was definitely one of the most feminine girls Dana had ever known. Boys seemed to want to cuddle Shelley, Dana thought, and that was kind of nice.

"What are you up to tonight, Dana?" Faith called from the landing.

"I made a rash promise, and I have to keep it," Dana said, grinning. "In a weak moment I told Terry I'd go see that monster movie with him."

"Dana! You hate monster movies," Faith said.

"True," Dana admitted, "But after all, Terry is a fellow Baker House roomie."

"Sure seems funny to have Sheffield and

Terry and Keith living here, even after all this time," Faith said.

"Don't stay out too late. We have to get up early tomorrow," Dana reminded Faith.

"I know, Greenleaf Memorial Hospital," Faith said. "I haven't forgotten."

"If we all set our alarms for six, one of us will get up," Dana suggested.

"It will take both of us to pry Shelley from her bed," Faith said.

"Faith! Your date is here." Terry's voice cracked through the hallway.

"That's Johnny," Faith said. "See you later, Dana. Have a good time with the monsters."

"Dana Morrison! Your extremely handsome, one-of-a-kind, too-good-to-be-true, all American male is here. Genuflect and pay homage, and then get down here."

Dana smiled and picked up her purse. Terry was announcing himself, and as usual, was teasing. "And Dana?" the booming voice called out again, "bring some money. I'm running a little short."

"How short?" Dana asked when she reached the bottom of the steps.

Terry was dressed in jeans and a pale blue sweater that contrasted nicely with his dark wavy hair and freckles. His smile was irresistible, and Dana found herself smiling back.

"Just a little short," Terry replied as he grabbed hold of Dana's arm and pulled her towards the door.

"How short?" Dana asked, thinking that

she sounded like a broken record.

"I've got some money," Terry announced. "Button up your coat, kid. It's freezing out there. And hurry, I talked Johnny into giving us a ride into town."

"Terry! How much money do you need?" Dana asked, pulling to a stop. "I'm not budging until you tell me."

"I've got about a dollar," Terry admitted. He pulled his ski cap over his head and hooked his arm through Dana's.

"In other words, it's my treat," Dana said as she ran beside Terry to Johnny's car.

"Think of it as a loan," Terry answered, his voice as cheerful as ever.

Terry O'Shaughnessy was a con man, but an irresistible one, Dana decided. She was actually looking forward to the evening. If anyone could take her mind off her sister, Maggie, the crazy Irishman could certainly do it!

CHAPTER FIVE

Faith's alarm clock was the first to start buzzing. She had deliberately placed the clock far enough away from her bed so that she would have to get up in order to turn it off.

"Come on, Dana, it's time to get up," Faith said.

Fifteen minutes later, both Faith and Dana, dressed in warm furry robes, peeled Shelley's gloves from her hands, dragged her from her bed, and guided her down the hall to the showers. "You got her toothbrush?" Faith asked Dana.

"Yes," Dana sighed, "and her towel, too. The things we do for you, Shelley."

Once Shelley had taken her shower, she was wide awake. She came back to the room and found that Dana and Faith were both dressed. Faith was wearing a navy blue skirt with a red sweater and matching knee highs, and

Dana was dressed in a pale blue skirt and blouse.

"Hurry, Shelley," Faith said. "Terry is meeting us in the lounge in a couple of minutes."

"What for?" Shelley asked.

"He signed up for hospital duty, too," Faith explained. "Now get moving, Shelley. Terry will start yelling at us and wake the whole house."

"I hope he found a ride into town for us," Dana said.

"Johnny offered but I wouldn't let him do it," Faith explained. "Saturday is the only day he can sleep in. Besides, the walk will be good for us," she added, trying to sound enthusiastic.

"Shouldn't we eat something before we start out?" Shelley asked.

"I don't think the dining hall opens until seven. We'll grab something in the hospital cafeteria if we get there early enough," Dana said. "Shelley, you don't want to wear the green skirt with that purple sweater."

"I don't?" Shelley asked.

"Wear your white sweater," Dana suggested.

Shelley shrugged her acceptance and pulled the white turtleneck sweater from the closet.

Terry couldn't find anyone willing to give them a ride into town so everyone slipped into boots, gloves, hats, and scarves and headed out into the bitter cold.

The girls were silent during the mile hike, but Terry kept up a running monologue, describing in vivid detail all the gruesome scenes of the monster movie.

When the hospital came into view, Shelley turned to Faith and asked, "What are we supposed to do?"

"We all have to report to Mrs. Donnaldson at eight on the dot," Faith explained.

"It's almost eight now," Dana said, checking her watch. "Sorry, Shelley, no time for breakfast."

"I'm not hungry anymore, anyway," Shelley replied. "Terry's gory description of the movie took my appetite away."

"It's a pretty building, don't you think?" Dana said to the group.

"Dignified-looking," Terry supplied. "Dignified and old."

"It looks old because it is old," Faith explained. She looked up at the five story structure. The all brick building was covered with ivy and Faith thought it was probably very pretty in the summertime, when the clinging vines were green instead of winter brown.

"We better move," Terry said. "It's two minutes 'til eight."

"Right. Let's get inside and find this Mrs. Donnaldson," Faith said.

It was an easy search. As soon as the foursome walked into the front lobby they met their new employer. It was simple to figure out who she was. Mrs. Donnaldson was standing in the middle of the reception area, a clipboard in her hand, motioning to them.

She was also the only person in the room.

Their new boss was just as imposing-looking as the building, Faith thought. She was almost six feet tall, ruler thin, with dark brown hair laced with gray secured in a rather austere bun at the back of her neck.

The woman's sparkling white uniform looked starched enough to stand up all by itself. Faith considered that she might have been a little afraid of the lady if it wasn't for the warm brown eyes with laugh wrinkles at the corners. Mrs. Donnaldson smiled, and the thought that she was imposing and austere no longer fit.

"Good morning," she greeted them in a soft voice. "My name is Mrs. Donnaldson and I'm the Patient Advocate here. For those of you who are not familiar with that title, I'll explain. I'm the go-between and problem solver. If a patient has a problem, I try to take care of it. I pamper them and try to see to all of their needs, other than medical, of course. Any questions?"

Shelley, Dana, and Faith all shook their heads but Terry did have a question. "Are we all going to work with you?" he asked.

"No, you all have separate assignments. This is the first year we are participating in Mr. Kimble's social involvement project and I have already decided who will work where. Mr. O'Shaughnessy," she said as she checked the clipboard, "you've been assigned to X-ray."

"You can call us by our first names," Terry

insisted with a grin that had Mrs. Donnaldson smiling in return.

"Fine. Now Terry, while you have been assigned to X-ray, there will be times when you won't be busy and then you'll help out in Pediatrics. X-ray is on the lower level. Just follow the signs and introduce yourself when you find it."

"Now which one of you young ladies is Shelley?" she asked.

"I am," Shelley immediately answered, pointing to herself. She was nervous and hoped that it didn't show.

"You'll be working the gift cart. Mr. Hamilton is in charge of the volunteers at the hospital, and he will explain everything you need to know. He's right down that hallway, on your left, and he's waiting for you. Off you go now."

Shelley nodded and quickly hurried away.

"Now I need Dana Morrison," Mrs. Donnaldson said.

"That's me," Dana answered.

"Dana, you've been assigned to work with our chief dietitian for Greenleaf, Ms. Janice Gordon. Her office is right next to the kitchen. Just follow the arrows and you won't have any trouble finding her."

After Dana left, Mrs. Donnaldson said, "That leaves you, Faith." She stopped suddenly and then added, "My, what a lovely name."

"Thank you," Faith said.

"You're the lucky one. You've been assigned

to me," Mrs. Donnaldson teased.

"That's great," Faith answered. "I hope I can be of some help . . . with the problems," she added.

"I'm sure you will. We have several calls to make this morning. Follow me and we'll see about storing your coat and purse. Then we'll get down to business." With those words, and another smile, Mrs. Donnaldson pivoted and started down the hall. Faith found she had to practically run to keep up. Mrs. Donnaldson was such a nice person that Faith felt completely at ease. She was eager to start her job, and hoped she pleased her new employer.

They reached what Faith assumed was Mrs. Donnaldson's office. When she looked around, and saw how spotless and organized the small cubicle was, she figured it had to be the Patient Advocate's area.

The phone was ringing and while Mrs. Donnaldson answered it, Faith took off her boots, pulled her loafers out of her king-sized purse, and hung her coat on one of the hangers hooked to the back of the door.

"Here's a white lab jacket to wear, Faith. Just put it on over your sweater, so you'll look nice and official. Until you get the hang of things, let me do most of the talking," she went on. "Then I'll let you make some of the calls all by yourself. I better warn you. You're going to do a lot of walking."

Mrs. Donnaldson opened the door and started out. "This isn't an acute care facility," she stated as they walked to the elevator.

"What does acute care mean?" Faith asked.

"Good question. That's medical talk for really sick people," Mrs. Donnaldson said with a wink. "If I get too technical for you be sure to keep asking me to explain. It's the only way you'll learn, and I'll know you aren't bored or falling asleep."

"Okay," Faith answered. "What happens to the really sick people if they don't stay here?"

"We transfer them into Boston. It's only an hour away and they have better, more sophisticated equipment to handle the difficult cases."

"I see," Faith said. "I have one more question, okay?"

"Shoot."

"If the patients have problems, why don't they just ask the nurses to help?"

"Another good question! The nurses are really overloaded with work, and sometimes the patients won't confide in them. That's why I'm called the 'go-between'. I work with the patients and the staff."

"I see," Faith answered. She adjusted her jacket when the elevator door opened and followed the Patient Advocate inside.

"Our first call is on John Emery. He's ninety-two years old and as feisty as they come."

"What's he in for?"

"He had foot surgery two weeks ago and he's anxious to get home. The doctor wants him to stay a few more days and he isn't too happy about that."

Mrs. Donnaldson led the way to room 218. The television was blaring and a tiny man was propped up in bed, surrounded by pillows. "How are we doing today?" Mrs. Donnaldson asked, her voice cheerful.

"*We* aren't doing well at all," the patient snapped out. His voice sounded angry and harsh, but Faith was quick to see the sparkle in his eyes.

The patient's attention turned to Faith and Mrs. Donnaldson immediately introduced her.

"Faith will be helping me on Saturday mornings, Mr. Emery. Now what can we do for you?"

"I couldn't eat a bite of breakfast. It tasted like sandpaper," Mr. Emery complained. He folded his arms across his chest and gave Mrs. Donnaldson a glare that dared her to contradict him. Faith automatically looked at the tray and saw that most of the food was gone.

"Are you still hungry?" she asked.

"Of course I'm hungry."

"Faith, Mr. Emery doesn't have a restricted diet, so he can have another tray. Would you please go down to the kitchen and tell Janice Gordon to see what she can do?"

"Yes, Mrs. Donnaldson," Faith answered. "I'll see if I can bring your tray back myself."

"That's a good girl," Mr. Emery said.

Faith hurried back to the elevator and pressed the button for the first floor. The door was about to close when she heard a deep voice call out, "Hold that door for me!"

Faith immediately pushed the button to keep the door open.

A tall black man, dressed in dark pants and a white lab jacket, entered the elevator and gave Faith a wide smile. "Thanks. I hate waiting on these things."

Faith tried her best to say, "You're welcome," but the words got stuck in her throat. The man standing right beside her was the most handsome person she had ever laid eyes on. She mumbled something she was sure he didn't hear, and looked straight ahead.

"You new here?" the man asked. His voice was deep and rich with a dreamy quality to it that Faith was sure could melt butter. It was certainly melting her!

"Yes," she finally got out. "Volunteer," she added. Her voice sounded clipped and harsh to her. "My name is Faith," she said, trying to soften her voice.

"Hello, Faith. My name is Frank Webster." He extended his hand and Faith shook it. He smiled again, and Faith felt some of her nervousness subside. His teeth were so even and white, Faith felt like asking him if he had worn braces. She caught herself in time. "Volunteer?" she asked instead.

"Doctor," he corrected. "Brand new. I'm working in the E.R. for six weeks. Part of my rotation," he explained.

Faith nodded, pretending that she understood. The door opened on the first floor and

Faith started out. "It was nice meeting you," she called as the door closed.

She was sure she heard "Same here", but then again, maybe she didn't.

Faith took a deep breath to try and calm her racing heart, and shook her head. What a crazy reaction, she thought as she headed to the kitchen. It certainly wasn't like her to behave like a dumbfounded ten-year-old! She prided herself on being cool and calm at all times.

After two wrong turns and one very helpful nurse giving directions, Faith finally found the kitchen. Dana and another person were standing just inside the door.

"How's it going?" Faith asked.

"Fine," Dana answered. "Ms. Gordon, this is my friend, Faith. Faith, meet Janice Gordon. She runs the place."

"Only the kitchen," Ms. Gordon announced.

Janice Gordon was a striking blonde with clear blue eyes. She had high cheek bones and didn't look more than twenty years old.

"What can we do for you?" Ms. Gordon asked.

"Mr. Emery would like. . . ."

"Another breakfast," Ms. Gordon answered. "It's all ready. Right over there," she said, motioning to the table.

"How did you know?" Faith asked, clearly puzzled.

"It's Saturday. He always has two breakfasts

on Saturdays and Wednesdays," she explained.
"He's crazy about our homemade rolls."

"Why didn't he just order a second breakfast?" Dana asked. "Or more rolls?"

"He'd have to admit he likes the food if
he did that," Ms. Gordon explained. "It goes
against his nature to admit he likes anything
here."

Dana and Faith both laughed. "He really
is nice," Faith said. "He had a big smile on
his face when we walked into the room. He
was watching television and something must
have tickled him, but as soon as he saw us, he
frowned."

"It's just a little act," Janice Gordon said.

"I better get back," Faith said. She picked
up the tray and started for the door. "It was
nice meeting you, Ms. Gordon," she called
over her shoulder. She stopped suddenly and
turned. "Can you tell me what E.R. means?"

"Emergency Room," Ms. Gordon promptly
answered.

"What does it mean if you're doing a
rotation?"

"That's when you go to several hospitals.
You do six or eight weeks at each hospital,
working in different areas. Why?"

"Oh, nothing. Just wondering," Faith said.
"See you later, Dana."

Faith didn't have time to think about Dr.
Webster for the rest of the morning. She was
busy meeting people and helping to solve
problems.

"Time to close shop," Mrs. Donnaldson announced at noon. "I've enjoyed working with you, Faith. I'll see you next Saturday."

Faith said good-bye and went back to the kitchen to collect Dana.

"Let's go eat in the cafeteria," Dana suggested. "I saw Shelley and told her to meet us there, okay?"

"Fine," Faith answered. "Should I go find Terry first?"

"Let's both go," Dana suggested. "X-ray is in the basement, isn't it?"

The two girls took the steps instead of waiting for the elevator and found Terry just coming out of the X-ray reception area. He was wheeling a little boy down the hall in a wheel chair that squeaked. "I have to take this guy back to the Emergency Room and then I'm done," Terry explained. "I'll meet you in the cafeteria."

"I'll go with you," Faith blurted out. She slowed down and added, "I want to see what the E.R. looks like, okay?"

"Sure," Terry replied, smiling. "Hang on, kid. I'm going to give you the ride of your life."

Terry was as good as his word, much to the little boy's delight. Faith had to jog to keep up.

They kept up the breakneck pace until they reached the entrance to the Emergency Room and Terry slowed to a snail's pace. He assumed a very sophisticated attitude when he delivered his patient to the nurse on duty.

While Terry talked to the little boy, Faith

strolled around the area, looking for Dr. Webster. He was nowhere in sight, and she found she was terribly disappointed.

"We meet again!"

Faith turned and bumped into the cause of her skipping heartbeat. "Hello again," she said, smiling.

"Want a quick tour?" he asked. He seemed eager to show Faith around and she was just as enthusiastic.

Terry joined them and after Faith introduced him, Dr. Webster spent most of the tour answering Terry's endless questions. Faith was frustrated and confused. She realized that she wanted Dr. Webster's undivided attention and felt absolutely ridiculous about it! She forced herself to pay attention to what was being said while she memorized each and every gesture the new doctor made.

"We have to meet Shelley and Dana upstairs in the cafeteria," Terry said. "Can you eat lunch with us?" he asked. "I want to hear all about medical school," he explained.

"Sure," Dr. Webster answered. "I have to wrap an ankle first, though. I'll meet you upstairs. Save me a spot," he said, looking right at Faith.

She nodded and followed Terry out of the Emergency Room. She was suddenly very glad that Terry had intruded. She certainly wouldn't have had the courage to ask Dr. Webster to eat lunch with the group, but Terry had thought nothing of it. Terry was so outgoing, so natural.

"You didn't mind that I asked him to join us, did you?" Terry asked as they waited for the elevator.

"Oh, no," Faith rushed out. "I think that was very nice of you." She felt like laughing! Mind? She didn't mind at all.

"I didn't think so," Terry said, grinning.

Faith frowned and looked Terry right in the eye. "Meaning?" she asked with as much of a frown as she could muster.

Terry shrugged. "Nothing," he finally said. "He's really a sharp guy," he praised, changing the subject. "He's not actually a for real doctor yet, did you hear him say that?"

"No," Faith answered. "I was —"

"Daydreaming," Terry supplied. "Anyway, he's a fourth year medical student. He graduates this term. The last six months of his schooling is spent going around to a bunch of hospitals to get some specialized training."

Dana and Shelley were waiting at the entrance to the cafeteria. "Look, you guys," Shelley said. She held up four tickets. "Mrs. Donnaldson gave each of us free meal tickets."

"That's great," Terry said. "I thought I'd have to borrow from Dana again."

"Terry, when did I become your Savings and Loan?" Dana asked.

Terry didn't answer. He handed each of the girls a tray and at their insistence started down the line before them. "I don't think you should have told him it was a free meal until after he ate," Dana said to Shelley.

"Look at all that food he's putting on his tray!"

"Disgusting!" Shelley muttered. "He eats like a horse and doesn't gain a pound."

Once they were all settled at a round table, Shelley told them all about her morning. "First I take the cart all around and give out juice, but I have to be real careful in case someone wants something they can't have." She paused for a breath and then continued, "Now 317 can't have any sugar so I have to give him a sugarless drink. There's a lot of responsibility with the job," she added, "keeping everyone straight."

"So after you give everyone their juice, then what?" Terry asked.

"I hand out magazines and sell candy bars. The money goes to the gift shop," Shelley explained. "And I visit with the patients. It's really fun."

"What about you, Faith? How was your morning?" Dana asked.

Faith quickly filled everyone in on her morning, ending with the statement that she really liked helping the Patient Advocate. "Mrs. Donnaldson is such a nice lady," she said. "And she's funny, too. She always asks the patient how 'we' are doing, and that makes them smile. I think she does it on purpose."

"So how did it go with you, Dana?" Terry wanted to know. He was inhaling his food and listening, too.

"I worked with the head dietitian. It's really a tough job with a lot of responsibility," she added. "Janice has to balance all the patients' meals."

"What do you mean 'balance'?" Shelley asked.

"Well," Dana said, frowning. "That patient in 317 you said couldn't have sugar? He is probably a diabetic so he can't have any sugar at all in any of his meals. And some of the doctors put their patients on low calorie, high protein diets, or one of a dozen other kinds of diets, and Janice has to figure all that out and still give them a well balanced meal."

"Sounds like she has to be a computer," Terry said.

"She uses one," Dana explained. "Just keeping track of all the different diets and still providing the four basic food groups is extremely important, to say nothing of the bulk everyone needs in their diets."

Faith looked at Shelley who looked at Terry, and then they all looked at Dana. "Four basic food groups? Bulk?" Shelley was struggling not to laugh because Dana seemed to be extremely serious, and she didn't want to hurt her feelings.

"Go ahead and laugh," Dana said, totally unaffected by their teasing looks. "I'm telling you guys that in the last four hours I've learned more about the junk food I've been eating, and how terrible it is and I've decided to change my ways. Janice says I should make a rule never to eat anything unless I know what's in it," she added in a voice that sounded like she was making a vow.

"That means you'll never be able to eat in the school cafeteria again," Terry said with a grin. "I never know what's in the stuff they serve us."

"Do you guys have any idea how many artificial ingredients the manufacturers put in things?" Dana asked. Before anyone could do more than shake their heads and glance at each other, she launched into a spontaneous lecture on the need for healthy food.

"Well you certainly sound convinced and very . . . enthusiastic," Faith said when Dana finally ran out of words.

"Our bodies are like finely tuned machines," Dana quoted.

"Sounds like Janice made quite an impression on you," Shelley interjected. She noticed that Terry was finished with his meal and was eyeing her pie with an appreciative stare. Shelley laughed and handed the plate to him. "Help yourself, Terry. All this talk about food has made me feel guilty taking two desserts."

"Good!" Dana's voice radiated praise. "Say, I've got this wonderful idea," she added with a rush. "For my paper, I think I'll figure out a good, healthy diet for all of us to follow. Are you guys willing to eat good, healthy food and cut out the junk for awhile? I'll make up a schedule of the food groups and —"

"Count me out," Terry immediately interjected. He had a funny grimace on his face and Faith couldn't help but smile. He acted like Dana was suggesting some terrible punishment.

"Faith doesn't need to lose any weight," Shelley insisted.

"This isn't a diet to lose weight," Dana explained. "I'm talking about a whole new way of life! No more junk food!"

"I can handle that," Faith announced. "And so can you, Shelley."

"Well," Shelley hesitated and then nodded. "Okay, Dana. You 'balance' our meals and we'll eat what we're supposed to eat."

"Promise?" Dana asked, giving Shelley a hard look.

"We promise," Faith answered. She glanced around the room again, hoping she would see Dr. Webster, but he was nowhere in sight. She thought she hid her disappointment well, but when she looked over at Terry, he winked at her and she knew that he knew exactly what she was thinking.

Faith quickly looked down at her tray of food and picked up her fork again. She was stalling because as soon as everyone was finished eating, they would want to head back to Canby Hall.

"Hey, here comes Dr. Webster," Terry suddenly announced. He waved to the doctor and Faith looked up to see the intern nod and smile. He hadn't forgotten!

"Wow, is he ever good-looking," Shelley said. "Who is he?"

"A new doctor," Faith announced to everyone. "He works in E.R."

Everyone watched as Dr. Webster threaded his way around the tables. He didn't stop until he had circled their table, so that he could sit next to Faith.

While Frank tried to eat, Terry grilled him with questions about medicine.

"There was this kid up in Pediatrics who has to have his tonsils out,". Terry told the doctor. "Funny thing is, I have the same symptoms. I hope I don't have to have my tonsils out," he said.

"Drop by the E.R. before you leave and I'll look down your throat," Frank suggested.

Faith didn't say much during the conversation. She was content to sit next to Frank and listen.

It ended all too soon. Frank headed back to the E.R., and a few minutes later the foursome went downstairs to see about Terry's throat.

"It isn't funny," Terry announced when they were all walking back to Canby Hall. "How was I to know I didn't have any tonsils? I must have been a real little kid when I had them out."

Everyone kept straight faces and nodded.

"I mean, I had all the symptoms. It was a natural conclusion," he excused, grinning sheepishly.

CHAPTER SIX

"Did somebody die in there?" Casey asked when Faith opened the door to Room 407.

"No, that's just Shelley singing," Faith explained with a smile. The smile quickly turned into a grimace when Shelley tried to hit a high note, and Faith hurried out into the hall and shut the door behind her.

"Why is Shelley singing?" Casey asked. Another high screech pierced their ears. "Tell me later, I can't stand it." Casey rushed off.

"Casey Flint, you come back here," Faith demanded.

Casey complied, a guilty look on her face.

"Shelley needs all the encouragement and help she can get," Faith explained. "She has to sing a song at the opening of Act I in the play and. . . ."

"She's in trouble," Casey announced with her hands covering her ears. "Good heavens, Faith, she sounds like Kermit the Frog."

"You're not being kind."

"I'm being honest," Casey told her. "Is that Dana's guitar I hear in the background?"

Faith nodded.

"How can she stand it?"

"Earplugs."

"Smart girl," Casey said. "Doesn't Shelley have any idea how terrible she sounds?"

Faith shook her head again. "I think she might be tone deaf," she said. "Look, Casey, I'm getting a real bad feeling about this play. Shelley is so sure she has the part all sewn up. I thought she did, too, until I heard her sing. Now I'm not so sure."

"She's still the best actress around," Casey said. "Maybe when the director hears her sing, she'll cut out the music altogether. How long is the song?"

"Long," Faith said with a sigh. "*Really* long."

"Think positive," Casey suggested. "Look, she'll probably get better. I mean it's obvious that she just started practicing, right?" Casey's voice was eager and hopeful.

"Wrong," Faith announced. "She's been at it for a solid week. Tryouts are in two more days."

"Well then, what we need is a plan of action," Casey suggested.

"What we need is a miracle," Faith contradicted. "Got any ideas?"

"Not yet," Casey admitted. "I can't think with all that racket going on. Let me think about it and get back to you."

Casey was backing down the hall as she spoke and Faith started laughing.

She went back into the room and exchanged a long look with Dana.

"That's enough for tonight," Dana told Shelley. "You'll strain your voice if you don't rest it a bit," she added.

"Well what do you think?" Shelley asked Faith. "Dana says I'm good."

"Actually," Dana said when Faith raised both eyebrows at her, "I said you weren't as bad as you were yesterday," she explained.

"Same thing," Shelley said with a shrug. She stood up and stretched. "I think I'll go say hi to Casey. Maybe sing the song for her."

"Good idea," Faith suggested, trying not to smile.

Once Shelley was gone, Faith plopped down on her bed and stared at a very depressed-looking Dana. "What are we going to do!"

"I don't know," Dana said. "She tries so hard and she really thinks she's doing a fine job."

"You're a good person to try to help," Faith said. "In fact, you deserve a treat. Let's get a pizza."

"Okay," Dana said. "I don't think pizza qualifies as junk food, but I'll find out Saturday. One can't hurt. Let's see if Shelley and Casey want to come along."

Faith started to laugh. "If Shelley is singing, I have a feeling that Casey would walk all the way to Boston if we suggested it."

* * *

An entire group walked into town. Johnny had called just as they were all leaving, and Faith suggested he meet them there.

Keith and Casey held hands all the way to Pizza Pete's, and Shelley and Dana and Faith walked behind them. "Why didn't you ask Johnny to come and pick us up?" Shelley asked. It had started to drizzle and Shelley was the only one not wearing a hat.

"He had some things to do," Faith explained. "But he'll drive us back home."

When Johnny showed up, he sat down next to Faith. The group was crowded into a booth, but it was cozy and warm, and no one complained.

"How is it going with Shelley's song?" Johnny whispered into Faith's ear when no one was paying attention.

"Not good," she answered. "She's trying, but. . . ."

Johnny took hold of Faith's hand and squeezed it. She automatically smiled up at him. Inside she felt a twinge of guilt. All week long she had thought only of Frank Webster and hadn't given Johnny a single thought. She couldn't seem to help herself. Why, if she didn't know better, she would have thought she actually had a crush on Frank! Impossible, she chided herself. She was too mature and levelheaded to have a crush on anyone.

"Earth to Faith," Dana sang out. "Are you there?"

"What?" Faith said, embarrassed. "I'm sorry. I didn't hear what you said."

"Obviously," Johnny said, grinning. "What has you frowning so?"

"Nothing," Faith answered. "Really."

"Does everyone want mushrooms?" Shelley asked.

The conversation became serious, and everyone argued over what they wanted on the pizza. Dana had made it very clear that it might be their last for a long time.

Every time Faith thought about Frank Webster, she immediately pushed his image from her mind and concentrated on Johnny. It was a difficult task.

She sat in the front seat, next to Johnny, on the way back to Canby Hall and waited until everyone had filed out of the car before kissing him good-night.

"Don't worry so much about Shelley," Johnny suggested. "She'll do all right."

"I'll try," Faith replied, feeling more guilty by the minute. She wasn't thinking about Shelley at all. Johnny leaned down and gave Faith a slow, sweet kiss. It was full of tenderness, just like Johnny, and Faith found herself kissing him back with just as much tenderness.

Her mind was a clutter of conflicting emotions. Shelley chattered while everyone got ready for bed, but Faith wasn't really listening to her.

She got into bed and welcomed sleep. Frank's face, so bronzed and distinguished-

looking with those wonderful high cheekbones, flashed before her eyes and Faith grimaced with frustration.

I'm disgusting! Faith thought. She had just
kissed Johnny, not twenty minutes ago, and
was now fantasizing how it would feel to be
kissed by Frank Webster.

Disgusting and fickle, she thought before
falling off to sleep.

Dana worked as often as possible with Shelley
and vowed to the disbelieving Casey and
dubious Faith that she had noticed some im-
provement in Shelley's voice. Not much, she
admitted to herself with real honesty, but
some.

She reluctantly went over to the administration building and picked up an application
for Maggie and mailed it to her mother with
a short note. She was going to have to do
something, and soon, she realized. The problem was simple. She didn't know *what* to do.
The knot grew inside her stomach, a constant
reminder, and she found herself getting very
angry with her mother and her sister, and
most of all, with herself.

Faith had become very quiet and withdrawn
lately and Dana didn't want to keep harping
on her problems. Something seemed to be
troubling Faith but she was being very quiet
about it as usual.

Shelley certainly made up for her roommates' thoughtful and quiet moods. She
talked nonstop, growing more and more ex-

cited about the play tryouts. Casey, Dana, and Faith all promised that they would come to the tryouts to cheer Shelley on.

The day finally arrived and it started out perfectly. The temperature was a sunny, golden fifty degrees. And Shelley couldn't have been in a better mood. She was so positive about everything, so optimistic!

Shelley *had* done a wonderful job. She had memorized all her lines and didn't pause or forget any of the gestures she had practiced. And the song she had to sing wasn't too bad either. Adequate, Dana decided as she listened to Shelley. Not super, but definitely adequate.

"You've got it!" Casey declared in a loud whisper when Shelley joined the rest of the girls in the back of the auditorium to watch the rest of the auditions. Shelley nodded her agreement and smiled from ear to ear.

And then little Elizabeth Kennedy, the last to audition, walked onto the stage. No one had ever heard of Elizabeth Kennedy. She had transferred in the middle of the year and was only a freshman to boot. With auburn hair, blue eyes, a petite figure, and twin dimples, she was extremely dainty and feminine-looking. Like a china doll, Dana thought. After hearing Elizabeth sing, Faith was impressed. She could have been on Broadway. She was that good! She sang the play's opening song with a clear strong voice that sent goosebumps down Dana's arms. It was surprising to see such a small girl belt out a song in such a powerful voice.

Faith didn't have the heart to look over at Shelley, but Dana did. Shelley was pale and looked like she was about to be sick by the time the song had ended.

Dana glanced over at the stage again and noticed that Tom was looking very surprised and pleased.

"She's probably a terrible actress." Casey whispered the encouragement and everyone, including Dana, latched onto that possibility with fervent hope.

"Right! She probably hasn't ever been in a play. She's only a freshman."

"True," Dana added. "Besides, freshmen never get the lead in anything," Dana reminded the group. "It's unheard of."

"Relax, Shelley. You look a little . . . tense," Faith said.

"I'm okay," Shelley answered. "Okay, everyone be quiet. She's about to start with her first line."

Everyone immediately quieted down and crossed their fingers. But as they watched and listened, all their hopes died. Elizabeth Kennedy might not have been in any plays before coming to Canby Hall, but she was still fantastic.

No one said a word when the auditions ended. Shelley was obviously upset. She held a Kleenex in her hands and was methodically tearing it to bits.

Finally Casey braved a few words. "When do you find out who got the part?"

"Now," Shelley answered. She looked

straight ahead, at the empty stage, and tried to smile. Tom was coming towards them and she didn't want him to think she was at all worried. After all, Elizabeth Kennedy, great or not, was only a freshman.

"I better go up and join the group and wait with them," Shelley decided.

"We'll wait here," Dana said.

Everyone's eyes were on the drama coach who was furiously writing on some paper. Five and then ten minutes passed before the coach stood up and made the announcement.

Without explanation, she announced that Tom Stevenson had the male lead and Elizabeth Kennedy would be his heroine! Shelley would be Elizabeth's understudy.

Shelley didn't take it very well. But then she wasn't very good at masking her feelings. As soon as Elizabeth's name was announced, a group of shrill-sounding freshmen jumped up and clapped and hurried to congratulate the girl. Casey and Faith were watching Shelley, but Dana was watching Tom. He certainly didn't seem too upset about his girlfriend losing the part. In fact, from the grin on his face, Dana was sure he was pleased that Elizabeth had won. She watched as he went over and shook hands with Elizabeth and said a few words to her.

Shelley stood off to one side of the group with her shoulders slumped. Dana finally got up enough courage to look at her and then wished she hadn't.

"We better go get Shel," Faith said. "She looks like she's about to burst into tears."

"She's already in tears," Casey corrected.

They filed out of the seats into the aisle when Shelley turned and started towards them. "Look, I've got to get out of here and be alone for a few minutes. I'll see you guys later," Shelley called in a choked voice as she fled past the girls. Tears were streaming down her face and no one could think of anything to say.

"Can you believe it?" Casey muttered as the three walked out of the building. "I mean, a freshmen of all things," she added, disgust obvious in her tone of voice.

"She was good," Faith said. "You've got to admit that."

"She was terrific," Casey said, "But that doesn't make it fair. She's only a freshman and Shelley has worked so hard. . . ."

"Did you guys notice Tom's reaction?" Dana asked, frowning.

"No. What do you mean?" Faith asked.

"Oh, nothing," Dana said. "I just wondered how he felt about it."

"Here he comes now. Let's ask him," Casey suggested.

"Have you seen Shelley?" Tom asked. He looked extremely worried and Dana immediately felt better. Maybe she had misread him. Her imagination was just probably working overtime, she thought.

"She wanted to be alone for a few minutes," Faith told Tom. "She took off in that direction," she added, pointing to the path that led to the woods.

"Thanks," Tom called over his shoulder as he took off running.

The girls watched him as he raced down the path. "I hope he can console her," Casey said with a sigh. "And I sure don't envy you guys."

"What do you mean?" Faith asked.

"Shelley's going to be a little difficult to live with, I think," Casey explained.

"We'll put up with it," Dana promised. "That's what friends are for."

CHAPTER SEVEN

Shelley ran until her sides hurt. She didn't pause until she had reached the far edge of the campus park. There was a bench nestled among the dormant apple trees and Shelley sat down. She finally gave in to her demanding tears, and the trickle turned into a flood.

Shelley wiped the back of her hands over her wet cheekbones. Tom was coming. She could hear him yelling her name and from the sound, he was getting closer. It wouldn't do to have him find her whimpering like a baby, she decided. She would act very calm and cool and pretend that the part hadn't meant all that much to her anyway.

Her plan failed. As soon as she spotted Tom, she started to cry again. He hurried to her side, sat down beside her, and put a consoling arm around her bent shoulders. "Oh Shelley, don't cry. It isn't the end of the world," Tom whispered against her ear.

"I just can't believe it," Shelley told Tom between sobs of despair. "I was so sure," she said. "The part should have been mine! I deserved it."

"I thought you had the part, too," Tom said with a sympathetic look. He leaned down and gently kissed her on the forehead and then reached into his pocket and pulled out a Kleenex. He dabbed at her face, wiping away the tears and smiling at her. "Don't cry anymore, Shelley. It tears me up."

She could tell that her tears were really distressing Tom and she tried to stop. "I'm acting like a baby," she told him, hoping that he would contradict her. She didn't want to act like a child, but she couldn't seem to help herself.

"Look, it's a heck of a disappointment," Tom said. She decided it was his way of excusing her behavior. He took hold of her hand and pulled her to her feet. "Let's walk for awhile. It's getting cold again."

Shelley nodded and let Tom lead the way. He held her hand and they walked in silence for several minutes, each lost in their own thoughts. Then Tom blurted out, "Shelley, you'll get through this. I promise."

He sounded so sincere that Shelley found herself smiling. "But we won't be able to practice together," she reminded him. She heard herself whining and hated herself for it. "And it's so humiliating, Tom. I mean, she's just a freshman and I'm *her* understudy."

"Hey! That's right." Tom seemed to have

just remembered that. "Look, we can still practice together. Really," he hurried to add when Shelley cast him a disbelieving look. "Since you're the understudy, you'll have to know all the lines, in case —"

"In case something happens to Elizabeth Kennedy?" Shelley asked. "Like maybe the plague or —"

"Come on, Shelley," Tom said. "Let's go back to the auditorium and —"

"No," Shelley interrupted. "I'm really not in the mood. You go ahead. I've got to study anyway." She pulled her hand away and backed up a step. "I'll talk to you tomorrow, okay?"

Tom gave her a long look, and then reluctantly nodded. "Okay, you can be upset tonight," he said, "But tomorrow I expect the old Shelley back. I'll call you."

Shelley nodded and started up the steps to the dormitory.

Tom had said that she would get through this disappointment. Shelley didn't agree. Not tonight, anyway. With another sob of despair, Shelley ran to her room.

CHAPTER EIGHT

She's driving me crazy!" Dana was jogging beside Faith, hurrying to get back to Baker House. It was drizzling outside, and there was quite a frigid nip to the wind.

"Now, Dana," Faith placated, "it isn't all that bad. Shelley's still a little upset."

"Upset is an understatement," Dana panted. They reached the steps to Baker House and Dana paused. "She's done nothing but cry for days," she continued. "If she keeps this up, and I have a feeling she's going to, then I think we ought to seriously consider renting her out for funerals," she stated with a shake of her head.

Faith couldn't help grinning. "What happened to, 'What are friends for? We'll stand by her,' and all that?" Faith asked with a raised eyebrow. "I seem to remember your pledge to —"

"That was before the flood started," Dana

explained. She followed Faith inside. "I've really tried, Faith. Truly! Every time I try to talk to her about the play, I set her off again. She's used enough Kleenex to build five Homecoming floats."

"She can't help herself," Faith said, excusing Shelley's constant tears. "She's been humiliated," she continued. "After all, she *is* the understudy to a freshman."

"I wonder if she cries during play practice," Dana said.

"We're drenched. Let's go upstairs and change clothes," Faith suggested. She started up the steps but paused when Dana didn't follow. "Come on. You can take it. You're a big girl now."

"Okay, but promise not to say a word about the play," Dana warned. "Talk about anything but that!"

"I promise," Faith said, smiling. "Poor Shelley! My heart breaks for her."

"My ears are ringing from her," Dana said. "She sure isn't a very quiet crier, now is she?"

They reached the door of 407 and Faith opened it. Shelley was sitting at her desk, a book in her lap. She was staring out the window, and Dana was relieved to see that her cheeks were dry. She wasn't crying!

"I still think you ought to talk to Alison," Faith continued as she walked into the room.

"Why does Faith think you should talk to Alison?" Shelley asked the question, frowning at Dana.

"We were just talking about Maggie again. Faith thinks I ought to tell Alison how I feel and see if she has any suggestions."

"Are you still upset that your sister might come here next year?" Shelley's voice sounded very exasperated, and Dana immediately felt her back stiffen.

"I still can't believe how you're reacting," Shelley accused. "She *is* your sister," she reminded Dana. "So it's a disappointment," she continued, when Dana refused to turn around. "You're certainly old enough to deal with it."

"Oh, really?" Dana whirled around, fire in her eyes. She put her hands on her hips and drew a deep breath. "I seem to remember that line before, Shelley. You also told me I should learn to handle my disappointments like an adult, right?"

"Yes I did, and I'm right," Shelley said firmly. She looked at Faith and then back to Dana.

"Well you ought to practice what you preach," Dana retorted. She took a step towards Shelley and gave her a good glare. She knew she was baiting Shelley but didn't stop. Worse, she was enjoying herself! Shelley, she decided, had it coming!

"And just what do you mean by that?" Shelley asked. She slammed the book shut and dropped it on the desk.

"You certainly don't take your disappointments like an adult," Dana quickly pointed out. "You've done nothing but cry and feel sorry for yourself since you lost the part in that play."

"That's entirely different," Shelley cried out. She jumped to her feet and imitated Dana's stance, placing her hands on her hips.

"Oh? And how's that?" Dana demanded.

"You know what I mean," Shelley stammered. "The play is the most important thing in my life." She was starting to sound very dramatic.

Faith watched and listened, shaking her head. She threw her towel down on the bed and leaned against the window.

"And independence is the most important thing in my life," Dana countered.

"That doesn't make one bit of sense," Shelley told her. "What does independence have to do with Maggie?"

"You wouldn't understand," Dana snapped out. "You're too wrapped up in yourself."

Dana's voice reeked of disgust, and Shelley felt tears forming. "Thanks a heap," she muttered. Dana's statement had really hurt and Shelley found that she couldn't think of a single retort. "You just don't understand," she finally got out, sniffling.

"You're right. I don't," Dana told her. She saw the tears and moaned, "Oh, no, here we go again." With that pronouncement, Dana glanced over at Faith and said, "I'm going for a walk." She slammed out of the door then, without giving Shelley another look.

As soon as Dana left the room, Shelley cried in earnest. Faith watched her without saying a word. She heard a sigh and realized it had come from her. She was caught in the middle and didn't know how to proceed. Should she play the peacemaker? Probably, she answered herself. But first she would let both of her friends cool their tempers. Neither would be very reasonable now. Tomorrow, she decided. Tomorrow she would have a talk with both of them.

Faith sat down on the bed. Was she the only one around here with any sense, she asked herself?

It was Friday night, and Faith was getting ready for her date with Johnny. She had chosen a pale blue pair of slacks and a matching turtleneck sweater, and was just putting the finishing touches on her makeup. Faith used very little cosmetics on her face. She was lucky, she realized. Her skin was clear and unblemished. A tinge of blue eyeshadow and some lip gloss, and she was done. Faith didn't consider herself a raving beauty, but as her little brother was fond of saying, she wasn't hard on the eyes either!

Faith was really looking forward to her evening . . . not only because Johnny was her special boyfriend and she enjoyed being with him, but also because she would be getting out of 407, or as Casey called it, the war zone.

Dana and Shelley weren't speaking. They were both caught up in their fury with each other, and from all the signs and indications, the war was escalating.

With sudden insight, Faith realized that by
lashing out at each other, both Dana and
Shelley were directing their anger and frustration at something other than what was
really bothering them. Dana wasn't so consumed with her worry over Maggie now. She
spent all her time fuming at Shelley. And
Shelley wasn't crying as much now. She was
too busy barking at Dana, via Faith of course.

If she heard "Tell her . . ." one more time
from either of her roommates, Faith would
scream. Being levelheaded and practical did
have its negatives, she thought. She wondered
how Dana and Shelley would react if *she*
suddenly started yelling and screaming.

"Telephone, Faith!" a loud male voice
called out. Faith recognized Terry's yell and
hurried out of the room.

"Coming," she called back. She assumed it
was Johnny on the phone. He was probably
running late and was being thoughtful by
calling her to tell her he would be there
shortly.

Terry was hovering by the phone, a puzzled
look on his face. "It's Dr. Webster," he announced in a loud whisper. "What do you
think he wants?" he asked.

Faith's eyes widened when she heard who
was on the phone and she shook her head. "I
don't know," she whispered back.

"Here," Terry said, handing the phone to
her.

"Hello?" Her voice sounded breathless and
her heart raced.

"Hi, Faith. It's Frank," Dr. Webster said. "You sure are hard to find. This is the third dorm I've called."

"Oh!" Faith's mind was full of confusion, and excitement. She wanted to sound very adult, very sure of herself. "What did you want?" she asked, and then grimaced at the way she had phrased the question.

"You mentioned last Saturday that you had a good camera and that you take pictures for the school newspaper, and I have a little favor to ask you," Frank explained.

"Yes?" It was all she could think of to say. She didn't even remember telling him about her camera, or taking pictures, or anything! Her mind had turned to mush on her, just when she needed to be sharp and clever.

"My mom and dad keep asking me for some pictures. You know how mothers are," he explained with a laugh. "Anyway, I was hoping you'd bring your camera along tomorrow and take a couple of shots of me and the hospital."

"I'd be happy to," Faith replied, enthusiasm radiating in her voice.

"Hey, I'll pay for your expenses," Frank hurried to add.

"Oh, no," Faith rushed out. "I have all the equipment. You don't have to pay anything."

"Then I'll take you out for dinner. Deal?"

Faith felt like fainting. It was too good to be true. "Deal," she whispered. She said good-bye and hung up the phone. She turned with a sigh and floated back to her room.

Dana and Shelley were both in 407, ignoring each other, when Faith walked in. Neither noticed the silly grin on Faith's face or heard the soft sighs. For once Faith was glad they were both so wrapped up in their own problems. She didn't want anyone to know how she was feeling about Frank Webster, and if either of them had been in a normal state of mind, Faith's behavior would have been noticed and questioned immediately.

Faith said good-bye and went downstairs to wait for Johnny. The front lobby resembled an airport, Faith thought. Teenagers were coming and going, and there was an atmosphere of happiness and excitement in the air. Friday nights were always like that.

Johnny came through the door and spotted Faith immediately. They just smiled at each other, since kissing was not allowed on the campus, and held hands on their way to the car.

The evening was pleasant and confusing. Pleasant because she felt warm and comfortable with Johnny and was genuinely happy to be with him. Confusing, because several times during the evening, when Johnny was talking to her and she should have been paying attention to what he was saying, she wasn't. Odd, she considered, she used to think she couldn't feel warm and excited about two men at the same time, but now she found that she certainly could. She thought that Shelley was the only one who could love two boys at the same time. Though that was a

little different, she reminded herself, as one
of Shelley's boyfriends was a good thousand
miles away. That certainly kept the complica-
tions down a bit.

Johnny and Faith stopped at Pizza Pete's
for a late snack and Faith's thoughts of love
and dating came to an abrupt halt. As soon as
they walked inside and saw that their favorite
booth in the back was empty, they headed
for it. Then Faith spotted Tom Stevenson.
She raised her hand and was about to wave
to him when she noticed that he wasn't alone.
Seated next to him, on the same side of the
booth, was Elizabeth Kennedy. Elizabeth was
so petite, and Tom was so large, that Faith
almost didn't see her.

Johnny spotted the twosome at the exact
same moment. "Uh-oh," he whispered to Faith.

"Uh-oh is right," Faith replied.

She tried not to stare, but she felt rooted
to the floor, until Johnny took hold of her
elbow and guided her to their booth.

"Does Shelley know he's dating someone
else?" Johnny asked.

"Now don't jump to conclusions," Faith
cautioned, glancing around Johnny to look
at the couple under discussion. "It might not
be a date at all. Maybe they just had a late
play practice," she excused with a rush. That
sounded pretty reasonable to Faith, once she
had said it, and she smiled. "Yes, it was probably just a late practice. That's Elizabeth
Kennedy by the way. You know, the girl who
got the part in the play Shelley had her heart

set on? Shelley's her understudy."

"Then Shelley would have to go to a late play practice too, wouldn't she?" Johnny was being very logical, a quality Faith usually admired. Tonight, because she knew in her heart that he was right, she became irritated with him.

"I'm sure there's a reasonable explanation, Johnny," Faith said. "Don't convict on circumstantial evidence."

"Sure," Johnny said. He whistled in the air. "The explanation is that it's a date."

"How can you know that?" Faith snapped.

"Because he's holding her hand and every time she says anything, he smiles. In my book, that qualifies as a date."

"Oh Johnny! I know you're right. Shelley doesn't know. I'm sure of it. This will really upset her."

Johnny didn't immediately answer. He looked back across the room at the pair.

"Maybe we should go over and say hello," Faith suggested with new hope in her voice. "And then maybe he'll explain that it isn't a real date or something." It was the best plan of action Faith could think of. She wasn't one to sit back and wait for things to happen. She was a doer, not a waiter!

Johnny shook his head. "I hate to squelch your enthusiasm, but I doubt it," he told Faith. He patted her hand in a tender gesture. "Look, if they're still here when we leave, then we'll stop by their table and see what happens. He hasn't even noticed us, Faith. He only has eyes for her. She's kind of cute, isn't she?" he couldn't help but say.

Faith shot Johnny a disparaging look and muttered, "Cute has nothing to do with it. Honestly, Johnny, sometimes you aren't very sympathetic."

"I'm just stating the facts," Johnny replied. "I feel sorry for Shelley, too. I just don't know what to do about it."

They ordered their pizza, a small one, as Faith wasn't very hungry anymore. She kept glancing over at Tom and Elizabeth all through the meal.

"Look," she said as she nudged Johnny, "they're leaving."

Johnny looked over and both he and Faith watched as Tom stood up and helped Elizabeth from the booth. He took an incredibly long time helping Elizabeth with her coat, Faith thought. Then he put his arm around her shoulders as they headed towards the door.

"That clinches it," Faith said with a sigh.

"Yeah," Johnny said.

"Are you finished yet?" Faith asked. "Do you think Mitchell's is still open?" she asked, referring to the little drugstore down the street.

"Probably not," Johnny answered. "Why?"

"I need to stock up on some more Kleenex for Shelley. She's going to need it," Faith predicted. *And earplugs for Dana,* she added to herself.

CHAPTER NINE

Shelley couldn't sleep. She sat on her bed in her pajamas and waited for Faith to get home from her date with Johnny. She had been acting like such a child! She was feeling better now, and wanted to apologize for the misery she had put Faith through.

She would apologize to Dana, too, if she ever came back to the room. Dana had left in another huff right after dinner, and that was almost five hours ago.

She had dreaded play practice this afternoon, but it hadn't turned out to be as terrible as she thought. Several people did glance her way during the two hour practice, but they gave her smiles of encouragement. It was kind of nice, she considered. Fellow actors banded together. It was a closely knit group and everyone really cared about each other.

Tom and Elizabeth were center stage for most of the first act. Shelley couldn't bear to watch them. She kept her head buried in her script, dutifully trying to memorize the lines. It was a futile endeavor. Her heart just wasn't in it! And who could blame her, she asked herself. She was starting to feel sorry for herself again and blocked the self-pity from taking over. At least, she remembered, praising herself, she didn't cry.

She consoled herself and dared to watch Tom and Elizabeth, glancing up just in time to see him embrace Elizabeth!

It's just a play, and they are only acting, Shelley told herself. Tom, she noticed, was really putting his heart into the scene. He gave Elizabeth a long, almost awestruck look and Shelley found herself impressed with his acting ability. She was usually right up there next to him, in previous plays that is, and this was the first time she could really observe him as the fine actor she knew him to be.

Shelley had turned her attention to Elizabeth and grudgingly admitted that she was talented. *I'm just as talented,* she thought with spite. Elizabeth had a strong, forceful voice that projected all the way to the back of the auditorium, and Shelley knew that would certainly please the drama coach. She constantly harped on projecting!

Act I ended with Elizabeth giving Tom a light kiss. Or at least that's what the script called for. But Elizabeth's kiss was anything but light.

Shelley felt her cheeks grow warm with anger as Elizabeth pulled Tom's head down and kissed him with a great deal of enthusiasm. The kiss didn't quite end when the coach called "cut" either. Elizabeth, Shelley thought as she steamed, couldn't seem to let go of Tom!

Poor Tom! Shelley was certain that he was embarrassed by Elizabeth's blatant display. She waited for Tom to look over at her so she could give him a compassionate smile, but he never did glance her way.

Elizabeth was one pushy freshman, Shelley determined. Someone would have to have a little talk with her, explain the situation. Since she was new to the drama department, maybe she didn't realize that Tom was going with Shelley.

Her rival couldn't seem to let go of Tom's arm. The practice officially ended and she continued to hold onto him like the vines on a tree.

Shelley stood up and saw Elizabeth was trying to drag Tom off to the side of the stage. Tom, gentleman that he was, smiled and meekly let himself be led.

"Tom?" Shelley called out.

Tom looked over at her, a fleeting expression of alarm on his face, and Shelley smiled. She motioned for him to join her, almost laughing out loud at how vulnerable and embarrassed he looked. Shelley knew Elizabeth was making him miserable.

Shelley waited while Tom leaned down and said something to Elizabeth and then hurried down the steps of the stage and over to where Shelley waited for him.

"Hi," he greeted when he reached her side.

"Hi yourself," Shelley replied. "You were very good today," she praised.

"Thanks," he replied. He glanced back at the stage where Elizabeth stood and then back to Shelley. "Look, I've got to go. I've got some . . . stuff to do," he added.

He couldn't seem to look at Shelley. And that puzzled her. Then she understood. Poor Tom! He was still embarrassed by the kiss and Elizabeth's brash behavior. She started to tell him that it was okay, she understood. It was only a play, not real life. But Tom was already backing away. "I'll call you tomorrow," he told her. "We need to talk."

"Hey, it's Friday, remember?" Shelley called out with a laugh. She and Tom always went out on Friday nights.

"I can't make it tonight, Shel. Rehearsing has got me worn out and I'm behind in my studies. I think I need a night to myself. But I'll call you tomorrow," he repeated. "Okay?"

Shelley nodded. "Okay," she answered hesitantly. Tom seemed nervous and Shelley was worried that all the pressure from school and the play was overwhelming him.

The door opened to 407 and Faith walked into the room, bringing Shelley back to the present.

"How was your date with Johnny?" Shelley asked.

"Fine," Faith said. "Just fine."

"Faith," Shelley blurted out. "I've got something to tell you."

"And I've got something to tell you, too," Faith said. Her voice was grim and determined.

Dana walked in then, gave Shelley an automatic exasperated look, and sat down. "I'm beat," she said.

"Dana and Faith, I have something I want to say to both of you," Shelley announced in a serious voice.

"Sure," Faith said. Her voice was eager. Maybe Shelley had already heard about Tom and Elizabeth and wanted to talk to them about it. She looked long and hard at Shelley and her hopes were dashed. Shelley looked too calm, and there wasn't a single tear in sight.

"I just wanted to apologize to both of you," Shelley said. "I've been acting stupid and I want you to know I'm not going to cry anymore. Dana," she continued, "I really am sorry. I haven't been much of a friend to you lately."

Dana was surprised by Shelley's grown up attitude. "No more crying?" she asked with a grin, the first real grin she had given in days!

"No more crying," Shelley said. "That's a promise. And I'll start my health diet right this minute. Okay?"

"You'll get rid of the Tabs, and potato chips and candy bars?" Dana challenged. A glint appeared in Dana's eyes and Faith found herself smiling.

"What about you, Faith?" Dana asked.

"I'm in," Faith announced.

"Well, there's no time like the present," Dana said as she stood up. "I'll just put all this junk food in a box and take it to Casey's room."

"Okay," Shelley said and then turned her attention to Faith. "Oh, Faith? What did you want to tell me?"

Faith tried to look blank. "I can't remember," she lied. "Dana, I'll help you take this stuff to Casey's room. Shelley, you start in on your hands. Here's your lotion," she added, throwing the plastic bottle over to her roommate. "We'll be right back."

When Dana and Faith were in the hall, their arms loaded with treats, Faith said, "We've got to talk, Dana. And fast!"

Dana turned and frowned at Faith. "What's the matter?" She automatically whispered in response to Faith's whisper.

"Shelley!"

"Hey, things are okay now. Shelley apologized," she reminded Faith.

"Johnny and I saw Tom with Elizabeth Kennedy tonight. They had a date," she rushed out.

Dana stopped in her tracks and sighed. "Does Shelley know? Of course she doesn't," Dana continued. "Guess that's the end of the truce," she added.

"Be serious," Faith urged. She started down the hall in front of Dana and neither said a word until they had unloaded their goods on a very appreciative Casey and headed back to their room.

"What are we going to do?" Dana asked at last. "Poor Shelley. Are you sure it was a date?"

"It was a date," Faith said. "Johnny and I saw them together at Pizza Pete's. The way they were acting, it was obvious they weren't just friends. I've got to tell Shelley."

"Not tonight," Dana said. "Let's have one night of peace and quiet," she suggested. "Shelley needs a good night's sleep. If you tell her now, she'll be up most of the night, crying. And we have to work at the hospital tomorrow. Wait until after work when we're all walking back to Canby Hall. I'll keep Terry busy while you tell her."

"Okay."

"That creep!" Dana muttered with disgust.

"Exactly," Faith replied, thinking it was the perfect description of Tom.

Shelley was just finishing her lotion ritual when the two girls entered the room. "I'm really tired tonight," she told them. "The past couple of days have been hard. Crying can be exhausting," she added with a giggle.

"How come you and Tom didn't go out tonight?" Faith asked. She tried to sound innocently interested.

"He was tired, too, and had some things he had to do," Shelley said as she adjusted her gloves. She missed the look Dana and Faith exchanged. "Don't forget to set your alarms. Hospital duty awaits. Good-night, you guys."

Both Dana and Faith watched Shelley fluff her pillows and get settled. "Oh, I feel so much better now that we're all talking to each other. Things are looking up."

"Think so?" Dana's voice sounded hoarse.

"Sure," Shelley said with a yawn. "The worst is over. What else can happen?" On that cheerful note, Shelley closed her eyes.

Shelley got a good night's sleep but her two roommates tossed and turned. They were both worried about Shelley, and she didn't have a clue. Once she was awake, showered and dressed, she was eager to face the new day.

"Hurry up, you guys," she urged. "I want to eat breakfast in the cafeteria." When Dana frowned, Shelley hastened to add, "A good, nutritious breakfast that is."

The three roommates tried in vain to get Terry to join their health diet all the way into Greenleaf, but he was having no part of it. "I get funny when I don't have my junk food," Terry announced.

"What do you mean by funny?" Dana asked. "You're already funny."

"I'll start grinding my teeth and foaming at the mouth," Terry predicted. "Just like that guy in the monster movie we saw."

"You already grind your teeth and foam at the mouth," Shelley said with a giggle. Before Terry could comment, she spread her arms wide, nearly knocking him off his feet. "Oh, what a glorious day. Don't you think so? Spring is in the air. I can feel it."

"Right," Faith said, though her voice

lacked any enthusiasm. "Dana, wait up for me," she added when the path narrowed and she had dropped behind Terry and Shelley.

"How come *I* have to tell Shelley about Tom?" she asked when Dana joined her.

"Because you're the one who saw him, that's why," Dana explained. "Hey, how come you brought your camera along?"

"Oh, Frank, I mean Dr. Webster asked me to. He wants me to take some pictures of him for his family," she explained. She felt flustered all of a sudden and hoped Dana hadn't noticed it.

The path widened again, and Shelley and Terry waited. The rest of the distance was spent listening to Terry's views on medicine. "Don't you think I'd make a terrific doctor?" he asked them, with complete lack of humility.

"Yeah, you'd have your patients in stitches," Shelley said. Her eyes widened with her clever words and she chuckled. "Get it? Stitches?" she snorted.

Terry, Dana, and Faith all groaned at Shelley's pun. They reached the entrance to the hospital and Dana announced that there wasn't time for more than a quick breakfast. She guided them through the cafeteria line, glaring at Terry when he took three sweet rolls and two helpings of scrambled eggs.

Faith and Shelley blanched when Dana put grapefruit sections on their trays. She allowed each of them one piece of whole wheat bread and a single poached egg.

"At least she's letting us have bread," Shelley whispered to Faith. Dana heard and grinned. "That's for bulk," she whispered.

Faith shut her eyes for a moment. "Honestly, Dana, you're really getting into this, aren't you?"

They were just leaving the cafeteria when Dr. Webster walked in. "Hey Faith! Did you remember the camera?" he asked with a smile that warmed Faith to her toes.

"I sure did," she told him.

"How about getting together at noon?" he asked.

"I'll come down to the E.R. when I'm finished," she told him. "I've got to hurry now or I'll be late."

"Okay," Dr. Webster told her. "See you then." He gave her arm a little squeeze and Faith felt like she was floating.

The morning passed in a daze of anticipation. Faith followed Mrs. Donnaldson around, a perpetual smile on her face. She was fortunate that none of the patients had serious problems because she didn't think she could *stop* smiling, no matter what the complaint.

Shelley's morning was more difficult. It took a good deal of willpower not to taste any of the candy bars she pushed around on the cart. She did help herself to three orange juices, thinking that they had to be loaded with vitamins and that Dana would certainly understand. Besides, the head of volunteers had insisted that she help herself to any of the snacks, as a kind of payment for her help.

Shelley saw Terry when she reached the Pediatric Department.

She dispersed the juice while she listened to Terry's rather outlandish recitation of the Big Bad Wolf and found herself laughing right along with the children whenever Terry tried to sound like Little Red Riding Hood.

One little boy, who looked around four or five years of age, sat on Terry's lap. The child had enormous green eyes and ruddy cheeks and Shelley thought he was adorable.

"What are you in for?" she asked when she handed the child his juice.

"A little eye surgery," Terry answered for the boy. "He got his patch off this morning and he goes home tomorrow," he explained.

She noticed that Terry was squinting at her and asked, "What's the matter with *your* eyes?"

"Things are kind of blurry," Terry explained, frowning. "Maybe I should have Dr. Webster look at them when we're finished. What do you think?"

Shelley nodded, concerned. "Maybe you need glasses," she suggested. "I've never noticed you squinting before," she added as an afterthought.

When Shelley's shift ended, she put the cart away and hurried down to the cafeteria. She was starving!

Dana was waiting at the head of the cafeteria line. "How did your morning go?" she asked Shelley.

"Fine. I'm really hungry, though," she

said. "I didn't eat anything all morning long," she added, very pleased with herself.

"Here comes Faith," Dana told her.

"Hi guys. Listen, I can't eat with you. I promised to take some pictures of Dr. Webster."

"What about your . . . uh, your talk?" Dana asked, stammering. She give Faith a hard look, trying to make her remember that she had to tell Shelley about Tom.

"What talk?" Shelley asked.

"Nutrition," Faith announced. "We were going to have a talk about food, weren't we?" she asked Dana. "And we will, I promise. You both eat with Terry and wait for me, okay? This shouldn't take too long. Dr. Webster has customers, I mean, patients waiting for him no doubt. He's a very busy doctor." She couldn't keep the praise out of her voice.

Dana gave her a funny look and then nodded. "All right. But don't eat anything. I'll get something to go for you. Something healthy."

"I'm really not hungry," Faith said. And she wasn't, she realized with a grin. Just thinking about spending time with Dr. Webster had consumed all her thoughts. Food was the last thing on her mind.

"Three meals a day, well balanced, of course," Dana recited. She watched Faith leave and then turned to Shelley. "Now then," she said with a sparkle in her eyes. "Let's find something wonderfully healthy to eat."

Shelley nodded, trying not to look too glum. She was in the mood for something wonderfully chocolate, but she didn't think Dana would go for it. Her dismay increased when she listened to Dana ordering both of them liver with onions.

While Shelley was wishing she was in Faith's shoes, Faith was hurrying from Mrs. Donnaldson's office where she had left her camera, down to the E.R. She didn't want to keep Frank waiting! Her heart raced with her feet as she hurried along.

She was mildly disappointed when she saw that Frank was with a patient. Disappointment turned to exasperation when she realized the patient he was examining was Terry O'Shaughnessy!

Dr. Webster was looking in Terry's eyes with a small instrument that had a tiny light in it. She walked up to the exam table in time to hear Frank tell Terry he was fine.

"That's good to know," Terry said with a sigh. "Since this morning my eyes have been acting real strange," he admitted. "But if you're sure everything is all right. . . ."

Was Faith imagining it or did Terry sound somewhat disappointed?

"Terry, everything is as it should be." Frank, Faith decided, was trying hard not to laugh and her curiosity increased.

She waited until Terry went off to the cafeteria and then asked Frank what he found so amusing.

"Terry," Frank explained. "He has all the

symptoms," he added with a chuckle.

"Then he's sick?" Faith asked, growing alarmed.

"Not at all," the doctor contradicted. He gave Faith a smile. "He's suffering pains of sympathy. Last week he worked with a patient who had bad tonsils and he immediately thought he did, too. This week he must have talked to someone with an eye problem and he —"

Faith's laugh interrupted his statement. "You mean he's making it all up?"

"Not really," Frank said. "It's real enough to him but he'll get over it, I promise. Most new doctors go through the same thing, thinking they have whatever their patients have. It's normal so don't worry. Some expectant fathers go through labor pains when their wives do, did you know that?"

"No," Faith answered. "That must be terrible for them."

"Very nonproductive," Frank laughed. "All pain and no gain for the husband — at least the wife produces a baby. Are you ready to take some pictures? I did tell you how much I appreciate this, didn't I?"

"Yes, you did," Faith said. She felt as if she was glowing like a Christmas tree inside, just from the sincerity in his voice.

She straightened her shoulders and assumed what she hoped was a professional attitude. She desperately wanted to impress him, she suddenly realized, so that he would consider her an equal and not a teenager. "Now then, where would you like to stand?" she asked.

"How about right here?" Frank suggested. He adjusted the white jacket and straightened his burgundy-colored tie. "Think I should have my stethoscope looped around my neck or would that look too conspicuous?"

"I think your parents would love it. Too bad we don't have a patient you could be looking at," she said.

"We'd have to get their permission. Too bad Terry left but I have a feeling, if he talks to any more patients, he'll be back."

Faith clicked the first shot right in the middle of Frank's laugh. "Just keep looking pleased with yourself," she said.

"So I look pleased with myself, do I?" Frank answered with another heart-stopping smile. Faith continued to take pictures, from every angle imaginable. She didn't dare tell him, but she was going to have two sets of photos done. One set would be for Frank's parents, and the other set for her. She thought he was probably very photogenic, he was too good-looking not to be, and she thought she had captured him to a tee.

"Now try to look serious," she said.

Frank immediately erased the smile and frowned. "Not gloom and doom," Faith protested, "just serious."

Frank complied. Faith took several more pictures, but the one she knew she was going to like the best was the last one. Frank was looking right at her, an intense yet vulnerable look in his eyes.

"All finished," Faith finally announced with reluctance.

"Great, let's go grab a bite to eat," Frank said.

Faith nodded and smiled. She waited while Frank signed two charts and told the nurse he was going to the cafeteria.

As soon as she and the doctor walked into the lunch room, Dana waved a greeting. Faith wanted to sit with Frank all by herself, and then felt guilty for feeling that way. She waved back and followed Frank through the line, barely noticing what she put on her tray.

"When do you think the pictures will be ready?" Frank asked.

"I'll develop them this week and bring them Saturday," Faith promised.

"How about if we go out to dinner Saturday night," Frank suggested. "I promised you dinner. Do you like Chinese food?"

"I love it," Faith answered. "But you don't have to take me to dinner. I really don't mind. . . ."

"A promise is a promise," Frank told her. "Unless you have other plans or a boyfriend who might take exception to an older man escorting such a lovely lady around!" He was teasing her, Faith could tell by the sparkle in his eyes, but she was too flustered to smile back.

"No problem," she said. "I'd love to go out to dinner with you. Thank you for asking," she added.

"Hey, you're doing me the favor, remember?" Frank said.

Faith tried to keep it all in perspective but it was difficult. She kept wondering if Frank was just interested in repaying her for taking the pictures or if he was actually interested in her as a . . . woman. The rational, logical part of her brain decided that he was just being kind and considerate, and a good friend. The emotional side hoped just the opposite. And neither side of her brain considered Johnny's feelings at all. There simply wasn't room.

CHAPTER TEN

"W ant to talk about it?" Dana's soft voice intruded on Faith's thoughts as they walked back to Canby Hall. Shelley and Terry were a good ten feet in front of them, both talking enthusiastically at the same time.

"Talk about what?" Faith asked.

"Dr. Webster," Dana explained. She smiled at Faith's startled expression and dropped her voice to a mere whisper. "I'm not blind, you know. And you are one of my best friends. You like him, don't you?"

Like is too mild a word, Faith thought. "He's very nice," she replied.

"Nice? He's handsome, virile, intelligent, and a lot more," Dana told her.

Faith didn't reply but she found herself smiling at Dana's apt description of Frank. They walked a bit further in silence and then Dana said, "So I was wrong? You aren't interested in him?"

"Dana, for heaven's sake, he's ten years

older than I am," Faith replied. "Besides, what would he see in a silly teenager?"

"You aren't silly and you know it," Dana protested. "Look, I'm sorry I brought the subject up. Let's forget I said anything."

"I'd rather talk about Frank than tell Shelley about Tom," Faith admitted. "It's going to break her heart."

Dana sighed. Inside she ached for Shelley too. "I know, but if she hears it from someone else, like Pamela for instance, it would be much more terrible."

"You're right. Pamela would love to hurt Shelley. It's her specialty."

Shelley and Terry stood at the intersection in the center of Greenleaf and waited. Dana looped her arm through Terry's and pulled him ahead. "Faith needs to talk to Shelley," she whispered. "Let's give them a little space."

"What's up?" Terry asked, glancing back over his shoulder at the twosome trailing behind.

Dana reluctantly filled Terry in on the facts about Tom Stevenson and Elizabeth Kennedy, knowing he would find out soon enough.

"That's terrible," Terry said with real anger. "First the poor kid loses the part in the play and now she loses her boyfriend."

"I know," Dana said, feeling more miserable for Shelley by the minute. Dana looked back over her shoulder and gave Faith what she hoped was an encouraging smile.

Faith saw it and smiled back, shaking her head. She was still listening to Shelley recite her morning and waiting for her opportunity to bring the subject around to Tom.

Shelley rambled on and on and Faith finally lost patience. They were almost back at Canby Hall. "Listen Shelley, there's something I think I should tell you," she blurted out. "Johnny and I saw Tom with Elizabeth Kennedy last night."

"What?" Shelley asked. The news sank in and she added, "Where?"

"At Pizza Pete's. Tom was with her, Shelley, and it was obvious that they had a date."

"No! You're wrong, Faith," Shelley said with a nervous laugh. "Who were they with?"

"No one else. It was just the two of them. I'm not wrong, Shelley but I wish I was. Tom was holding her hand and . . . everything."

Shelley was too stunned to immediately react.

She felt like her world was crashing around her and she tried to stifle the sobs that rose in her aching throat. It didn't work, and before she could control herself, the tears were cascading down her cheeks.

"You are right, Faith. I saw how he acted at play practice and wouldn't admit it to myself. He was like a puppy running after Elizabeth. Oh, what am I going to do?" she cried.

"I don't know, Shelley," Faith said. She handed her friend a Kleenex and patted her on the shoulder.

"What would you do?" she asked.

Faith had to wait until the sobs had lessened a little so that Shelley could hear her answer. "I don't think I'd cry," she admitted. "But I would get good and mad. Then I'd tell myself it wasn't the end of the world and that there were plenty of other boys out there and —"

"But I'm not you!" Shelley wailed louder.

"I don't think she's taking it well," Terry told Dana when Shelley's sobs reached them.

Shelley didn't wait for Tom to call her. As soon as she got home from the hospital, she dumped her coat and gloves and marched to the phone.

Tom answered on the second ring. "Tom, it's Shelley," she began without hesitation. "I need to talk to you."

"I need to talk to you, too," Tom said. His voice sounded muffled over the line and kind of lifeless.

Shelley wasn't deterred by his lack of eagerness. Why, he had probably heard the rumor too. Shelley thought she might be grasping at straws, but she didn't care. It had to work out! It had to be okay.

"How about this afternoon? I could come over in an hour or so and we could go for a walk." Tom was hesitating over every word and Shelley felt her heart plunge to her stomach.

"That would be fine," she said. "I'm looking forward to it."

An hour turned out to be an eternity. Shelley changed into a pair of designer jeans with tapered legs that made her look almost thin, and wore a soft pink sweater. Dana loaned her a pink and green silk scarf to tie around her neck, and told her she looked quite fashionable.

She combed her hair again and again, until her scalp started to tingle in protest, and then decided to wait for Tom in the front hall. Both Faith and Dana asked if she wanted them to wait with her, and Shelley smiled.

"Thanks but no thanks," she told them. "It'll be okay, you'll see," she told them, trying her hardest to sound like she really meant it.

But it wasn't all right. It was over. Tom didn't even take hold of her hand when they walked through the campus. He kept his head downcast and very calmly told her the truth.

"I went out with Elizabeth last night and I've got another date with her tonight. I'm sorry, Shelley, I should have told you before I asked her out but it just sort of developed. I still really care about you but Elizabeth is. . . ."

"Different?" Shelley asked, trying to get him to look at her.

"I guess." Tom sounded miserable and Shelley found some grains of satisfaction in that.

"You should have told me," Shelley agreed. "I thought we had agreed not to date anyone else. I guess the rules have changed. Do you like her a lot?" As soon as the question was out of her mouth, she wished she hadn't asked it. Of course he liked her. He wouldn't be dating her if he didn't.

"You don't have to answer that," Shelley said. She turned back towards her dormitory and Tom quickly followed.

"Look, Shelley, I really think we should date other people. We're too young to get serious," he argued. "I still want to take you out, too. I care about you. You must know that!"

Shelley's eyes blinked to keep the tears from starting again. She nodded and continued to walk, not saying anything.

"Are you real angry?" Tom asked.

"Angry does not describe my feelings," Shelley muttered. She came to a stop and whirled around to face him. "Elizabeth Kennedy makes me want to scream. First she takes my part in the play and now she takes my boyfriend. She'll probably move into my room next! Angry?" she said in a louder voice. "Never. Why I'm positively intrigued. I just can't wait to see what she does to me next."

"Elizabeth isn't like that," Tom defended. "Everyone loves her. She's one of the nicest, sweetest girls on campus."

"If you think I'm going to stand here and listen to you praise her, you're crazy."

It was a great exit line but Shelley thought she ruined it when she tripped over her shoes on the way up the steps to Baker House.

Tom grabbed hold of her shoulders to steady her. "Shelley? Please don't be upset. I. . . ." He acted like he didn't know what else to say. "Look, I'll see you at play practice, okay?"

"Sure," Shelley answered. She couldn't look at him. She nodded just to have something to do, and hurried on.

"Maybe she'll come down with the plague or something," Casey said with a great deal of sympathy after listening to Shelley rant and rave about her new arch enemy, Elizabeth.

"With my luck, I'll be the one who gets the plague," Shelley muttered. Then she started to cry, and Casey found a hurried excuse for leaving Room 407.

She ran into Dana on her way back to her own room. "I'm going to declare 407 in official mourning," Casey announced before Dana could even say hello.

"Shelley crying again?" Dana asked with a frown of worry.

"Yeah," Casey admitted. "Who can blame her? I wish she'd get a little spunk though."

"Everyone handles their problems differently," Dana said. "At least Shelley isn't holding it inside like some of us do," she added, thinking of herself and the constant knot she carried around in her stomach when she thought about Maggie.

"Come with me," Casey suggested. "Give Shelley a little time to herself. I'll treat you to a Tab or something."

"Nothing artificial," Dana declared. She laughed when Casey grimaced.

"Maybe I can dig up an apple for you," Casey suggested. "Is that healthy enough?"

Monday morning, in the cafeteria, Shelley and Dana and Faith all found a little comic relief. It was, as Casey predicted, the day of the uniform, and Pamela *had* to wear it.

"She doesn't look too happy," Casey told the girls when she joined them at the table.

"You've seen her?" Shelley asked.

"In the cafeteria line."

Everyone immediately looked up and waited. A minute later Pamela appeared, or rather, stomped into the room, holding her tray of food. She was wearing a brown and white pleated skirt, a long sleeved white blouse, and a brown vest.

No one said a word, not even when Pamela paused at their table and gave them all a glare. "Well?" she demanded in a tight voice.

"Well what?" Casey asked.

"Well, what do you think?" Pamela insisted.

"It's nice," Faith told her. "Does the skirt have pockets?" she asked, trying to sound sincere.

"It's gross and you know it," Pamela snapped out. "Shelley, I heard that Tom is dating that cute freshman. She's the talk of the campus, you know. Everyone thinks she's really terrific. And so terribly talented. You know she took the lead in the play. No com-

petition I heard," she added with a smug
smile.

Dana's back stiffened. "Is the material
polyester?" she asked Pamela.

"What?" Pamela looked a little nonplussed.

"Your lovely outfit. Is it wash and wear?"
she asked.

Pamela, Dana was sure, had never owned
anything that was wash and wear. It wouldn't
have been rich enough, elegant enough.

The stab got to Pamela, Dana was pleased
to see. She gave them all one last glare and
turned away.

"I hate that uniform!" Shelley's announcement was said with vehemence. For some
reason, her comment made everyone laugh.
Shelley soon joined in.

"What's everyone doing after classes?" Casey
asked.

Dana answered first. "I have chorus practice."

"I'm going to go over to the photo lab and
develop some film," Faith said.

"I've got play practice," Shelley said. The
smile left her face with her statement.
"Maybe I'll miss today. I'm just the understudy."

"Don't," Dana advised. "No matter how
hard it will be for you, I think you should
go."

"Why?" Shelley asked.

"Because everyone will think you're not a
real trooper and that you're feeling sorry for
yourself. You wouldn't want that."

"I wouldn't?" Shelley asked, not really caring what anyone thought.

"No, you wouldn't," Faith chided. "You're through with feeling sorry for yourself, got that?"

"I was thinking about quitting if you must know," Shelley told the group. "My heart just isn't in it. Being an understudy is boring."

"But you might have to go on if anything happens to Elizabeth," Casey said. "I mean, she might break a leg or something."

"I wish," Shelley muttered.

"Shame on you, Shelley. You didn't mean that. You're just upset." Dana's voice was calm and soothing.

"No, I didn't mean it," Shelley admitted. "About anything happening to Elizabeth that is. I do want to quit."

"Well you can put that thought right out of your mind," Dana stated with emphasis. "No one in 407 is a quitter."

"That's the truth," Faith said. "Today is the start of a whole new week and —"

"How will I ever get through it?" Shelley said with a groan. "Seeing Tom with Elizabeth and knowing that everyone knows he's dating her. . . ." She sputtered to a stop and her eyes filled with tears.

Dana groaned. "Don't you dare cry," she told Shelley. "Enough is enough! You've cried enough tears to fill Lake Michigan. If you keep this up, I'll do something drastic. I promise."

"I don't cry on purpose," Shelley said with a sniff.

"That's fine," Faith placated. She gave Dana a look that said calm down and patted Shelley's hand. "Now Shelley, put a smile on your face and try to keep it there, no matter what happens today. Okay?"

Faith sounded so sincere and earnest that Shelley was hard pressed not to comply.

She smiled. "I'll try. I promise."

"That's the spirit," Faith praised. "It's all going to be smooth sailing from now on."

No one noticed Faith cross her fingers under the table.

CHAPTER ELEVEN

Dana ran into Shelley twice during the school day, and each time the very emotional roommate was dabbing at her eyes. Dana's patience was quickly fading. She almost blew her top when she saw Shelley munching on a Snickers candy bar.

Shelley at least had the good grace to act embarrassed. She handed the offending candy to Dana without a word and hurried off to her next class.

Dana was late from chorus practice. She dragged her guitar up to her room and found herself pacing the confines of the room. Both Shelley and Faith were absent, but Dana didn't welcome the solitude. When she was alone, and not dealing with Shelley's problems, she had time to think about Maggie. She still didn't have any answers, and that frustrated her. Dana admitted that she was a "do-er." Whenever a problem presented itself, she wanted to immediately set about fixing it! How could she fix Maggie? How could she change her own attitude?

She thought about what Faith had suggested, talking to the housemother about her problem, and suddenly that idea didn't sound so awful. Maybe Alison could give her a few suggestions. At least she didn't have the worry that she would condemn Dana for her attitude. Alison just wasn't like that. She never judged anyone. With new resolve, Dana put on her tennis shoes and headed for Alison's apartment.

Alison's domain was located in the attic of Baker. Right outside the door was a giant bulletin board cluttered with announcements of coming events and rules and regulations. Dana took a minute to check the weekend sign out sheet just to see who was going home. She realized she was stalling and finally got up the courage to knock on the door.

It wasn't that she dreaded talking to Alison. No, Alison was far more than a housemother. She was a friend as well. It was the topic of the conversation that Dana dreaded. Maybe now wasn't such a good time, Dana thought. She turned around and was about to head back to her room when the door opened behind her.

"Hi there, stranger," Alison called out.

Dana turned around and grinned. Alison was wearing a pair of jeans and a white smock top with a design of a parrot on the front. She was barefoot and didn't look much older than

Dana. It was a fact that Alison, at twenty-six, was one of the youngest housemothers around, and no doubt the prettiest. Her reddish brown hair was loaded with natural curl and Dana thought she always looked fashionably disheveled. "Have you got a few minutes?" Dana asked. "I'd like to talk to you about something."

"Of course," Alison told her. "Come on in. I'll fix you some hot tea. Make yourself comfortable while I fix it. Word's out you're into health food," Alison added approvingly, as she walked into the kitchen.

"Who'd you hear that from?" Dana asked.

"Casey, who else?" Alison called out, laughing. "I get all my information from her. How is Shelley handling the change in eating habits?" Alison called from the kitchen.

"Not well. I had to wrestle a candy bar out of her hands today. I didn't have the heart to lecture her though. She's really going through it right now and nagging her about a healthy diet wouldn't be very appropriate."

Alison came back into the room carrying a tray that held a china tea pot and two dainty cups. She poured Dana a steaming cup and handed it to her and then got settled on the sofa, across from Dana. "I heard about Shelley. Is she still very upset about the play?"

"Yes. And now Tom is dating the girl who got the part. Shelley isn't handling that well at all. Funny thing is," Dana said with a frown, "she's writing letters to Paul . . . that's her boyfriend back home, remember? Anyway, she's writing to him all the time and acting real homesick."

"That's natural," Alison decided. "But, tell me, Dana, are you here to talk about Shelley or yourself?"

Dana cleared her throat and said, "Well, actually, I am having a little, um, difficulty right now. Maybe you can give me a change in perspective."

"I'll try," Alison said.

Dana immediately launched into the story of Maggie coming to Canby Hall and her feelings about it. "I really don't want her to come and I feel really bad about that. Maggie is sweet but she's my little sister. And Canby Hall belongs to me. I wish she'd find her own boarding school! There, I've told you. Do you think I'm terrible? Shelley does."

"How does Maggie feel about all this?" Alison asked. "And no, I don't think you're terrible."

"How does Maggie feel?" Dana frowned, thinking over the question.

"So far you've told me that your mother wants her to come here. How does your little sister feel?"

"Probably pleased," Dana said.

"You think you're going to lose your new found independence, don't you?" As usual Alison homed in on the problem with acute accuracy.

"Yes. I'll have to watch out for Maggie, be responsible for her and. . . ."

"Dana, I've got an idea." Alison smiled and Dana felt a glimmer of hope take hold. "Why don't you call Maggie and invite her up here for a weekend? Spend some time with her and —"

"Talk her out of coming here? That's a great idea," Dana said happily.

"Hold on," Alison said. "No, I don't want you to talk her out of coming here. Just find out how she feels. Maybe you two can come to some resolutions."

Dana nodded. "You're right. I've never had the chance to talk to Maggie. Mom said Maggie was excited but. . . ."

"Call her tonight and invite her up."

Dana nodded. For the first time in weeks she felt like she had a handle on the situation. It might not work out the way Dana wanted it to — Maggie might still come to Canby after their talk, but at least Dana was *doing* something about the problem. If Maggie was insistent about following in her big sister's footsteps, then perhaps they could come up with some ground rules or something.

She and Alison talked for a few more minutes and then Dana thanked her for the tea and headed back to her room. Both Shelley and Faith were sitting at their desks. Faith was studying with an opened book in her lap and her chair tipped back at a precarious position, and Shelley was just staring out the window.

"Okay you guys, listen up," Dana announced with as much cheerfulness as she could summon up. "There's going to be some changes around here, starting now!" She looked at Faith and then at Shelley. "Anyone have a problem with that?"

"Depends on the kind of changes you have in mind," Faith said. She grinned at Dana and closed her book. "What *do* you have in mind?"

"Anything and everything," Dana said. She kicked off her shoes and sat down on the bed. Her cheeks were bright red from her run, her eyes bright with her new resolve. "For what seems an eternity, Shelley and I have been moping around," she began, deciding not to bring up Frank's name and Faith's withdrawn attitude. Faith would get the message without Dana being specific, she thought.

"I took your suggestion, Faith, and talked to Alison about Maggie. She suggested that I invite Maggie up for a weekend and I'm going to do just that. Maggie and I will have to come to terms about her coming here and that's that."

"You'll hurt that poor girl's feelings if you tell her you don't want her to come here," Shelley said, shaking her head.

"No, I won't," Dana said. "Because I'm going to tell her *why* I don't want her to come. I'll talk about independence and the responsibilities of being a big sister and hopefully she'll understand. If she doesn't, I'll have to set some rules, I guess, and learn to live with the situation. But I *won't* be moping around any longer, worrying about it and feeling guilty."

"Good!" Faith practically shouted the word.

"Now then," Dana continued. "This room is the pits. Shelley, you're going to change your attitude, too. No more talk about missing your family and not more than one letter to Paul a day. Got that?"

"Dana, I don't think it's your place to tell me what to do," Shelley protested in a small, timid voice.

"I care about you, Shelley, so that gives me the right," Dana argued. "And you're about to begin playing the most difficult role you've ever had. You're going to be cheerful and laugh *no matter what!*"

"Why? If I can't be miserable here, where can I be miserable?"

"That's just it. Misery is out."

"I *am* trying not to be miserable," Shelley said. "I went to play practice today, even though I didn't want to," she reminded both roommates.

"How was it?" Faith asked. Her voice was gentle, and Shelley started to cry again.

"It was terrible," Shelley confessed. "Elizabeth couldn't keep her hands off Tom and everyone knew before the practice was over that he had dumped me for her. How was it? It was humiliating. And you want me to smile?"

"Yes, I do," Dana insisted.

"Shelley, you should be very proud of yourself. You went to practice and . . . you didn't cry, did you?" Faith couldn't keep the alarm out of her voice as she considered that possibility out loud.

"I did not. I wouldn't cry in front of the other actors and actresses. We're professionals!"

"Good for you," Dana praised. "And there's another thing you should be proud of," she continued. "You've really been good about our new health diet."

"I ate half that candy bar before you insisted that I hand it over," Shelley reminded Dana.

Dana turned to Faith and grinned. "I had to pry it out of her hands," she said.

Shelley started to giggle and both Faith and Dana looked at her with amazement.

"See, you're smiling. That's a start!"

"I think I'll go say hi to Casey."

Dana immediately knew what Shelley was up to. "I'll tag along," she insisted. She laughed at Shelley's disappointed expression she couldn't quite hide. "I know you like a book, Shelley. If you think you're going to go to Casey's room and fill up on junk food, you're sadly mistaken." She linked her arm through Shelley's and pulled her out the door. "I'll read you some of the labels so you can hear about some of the artificial junk they put in. . . ."

Alone at last Faith pulled the file folder out from under her pillow and opened it.

Very carefully she spread the pictures of Dr. Frank Webster across the bed. There were ten of them, and every single one was wonderful. She had been right. Frank was very photogenic. Faith just stood there, staring at the photographs for long, silent minutes. *I won't take them with me to the hospital Saturday. I'll wait until our date and then show them to him. I'll give them to him then.*

She heard voices in the hall and rushed to gather the pictures. Then she placed them in her desk. The voices didn't stop at 407, and Faith breathed a sigh of relief. She wanted a little more time alone, so that she could think about Frank. She stretched out on the bed and closed her eyes. What would she wear Saturday night? she asked herself. She went through the list of outfits and finally decided on the long sleeved white wool dress. Yes, she thought, that dress would do nicely. She wanted to look very sophisticated and the white wool was just the thing.

Shelley got through the week without shedding another tear. It was quite an accomplishment and she found herself feeling very proud. Maybe Dana was right. Maybe she needed a complete change in attitude. Moping certainly hadn't helped any.

Besides, being cheerful did have some benefits, some perks. The other drama students now considered Shelley very courageous and remarkable, Shelley thought. She was sure they did! Each day at play practice, whenever Tom and Elizabeth would embrace or share a special smile with each other, Shelley would feel her fellow actors glance her way. She would then plaster a smile on her face and force herself to keep it there. Inside, she felt like throwing up, she admitted, but they certainly didn't need to know that.

Yes, she was plenty miserable inside and it took all she had to keep the smile in place and not let anyone know how she really felt. It was, as Dana had predicted, her greatest and most challenging role. Shelley secretly thought she was a lot like one of those desolate, but beautiful, heroines in a Shakespearean tragedy.

By the time Friday afternoon came, Shelley sighed with relief. Playing Miss Merry Sunshine all the time was exhausting! She glanced at her watch and realized she only had one half hour left of play practice and then two glorious days off. She sat with the other drama students and watched Tom and Elizabeth on stage with the drama coach. And all the while, she smiled. She was sure her facial muscles were going to lock in position but she kept it up. Shelley wasn't really paying much attention to the directions the drama instructor was giving, until she heard a protest. They were working on the second act, and it wasn't going well.

"I think you're wrong," Elizabeth shouted at the coach. "The character should still be sad, not happy, and that's how I'm going to play her. I am the star, remember!"

Shelley could not believe what she was

hearing and seeing. Elizabeth stood in the center of the stage with her hands on her hips, and actually had the audacity to glare at the drama coach while she stomped her foot on the wooden floor.

Shelley was dumbfounded! Elizabeth Kennedy was showing a new side to her disposition and was, without a doubt, having a tantrum! Shelley knew her mouth dropped open in astonishment as she watched Elizabeth declare that she was finished for the day and march out of the auditorium.

She turned her attention to Tom and smiled the first natural, for real, smile in days. Tom looked stunned!

"Looks like E.K. has a bit of the prima donna streak in her," one of the actors muttered to Shelley.

"Sure seems that way," Shelley replied, trying not to sound so darn happy about it.

"Can you believe how she yelled at the coach?" another voice whispered.

The drama instructor clapped her hands and everyone immediately quit talking.

"It's Friday and everyone is tired. We'll break for today. Be here after school on Monday and have a nice weekend."

"Can you beat that?" another voice, sounding incredulous, said.

Shelley didn't turn around but she continued to listen. "The coach is going to let it pass."

"Did you hear Elizabeth? What's the matter with her?"

"What about the coach? 'Everyone is tired?' Ha! That's just her way of excusing Elizabeth's behavior," another voice stated.

Shelley decided it was best not to get involved. She gathered her things and put on her coat. "See you all Monday. Have a nice weekend," she called out as she headed for the door.

"Shelley, wait up." Tom's voice stopped her in her tracks. Shelley turned around very slowly so that she wouldn't appear overly eager, plastered a polite smile on her face, and waited.

"How have you been?" Tom asked when he reached her. Shelley thought she heard some anxiety in his voice but she couldn't be sure.

"I've been fine, Tom. Busy," she said.

The smiling became more and more difficult to hold. Tom was the reason. He looked so handsome and sweet standing there, hovering over her. Odd, she thought, he didn't look so self-assured now. Why, he looked kind of vulnerable!

Tom continued to stare at her, shifting from one foot to the other. Shelley couldn't bear the silence a second longer. She felt like she was in a staring contest, and losing. "So, what's new with you? How have you been?" Her voice sounded strained and not as cheerful as she had planned.

"Okay," Tom said, dragging the word out. "I was wondering if you had plans for this evening. I've really missed you and I thought we could get together."

"I'd like that, Tom," Shelley answered, "but I have other plans." She was lying through her teeth and hoped he couldn't tell. Shelley wasn't very good at lying.

Tom looked disappointed and Shelley wanted desperately to change her mind. She couldn't, of course, for two very important reasons. The first was the fact that she had seen Elizabeth say something to Tom right before she stomped off the stage, and she concluded that the freshman had broken their date. Even if that wasn't the case, Shelley wasn't about to accept a date with only two hour's notice. She refused to be a substitute, she told herself. The other reason for her refusal was just as important. Dana would have killed her if she'd accepted!

"Look, Tom," she blurted out before she had a change of heart, "I've really got to run. It was nice talking to you. Maybe I'll see you at the next mixer or something," she mumbled. Then she lowered her voice and gaze, staring at the third button on his blue vest. "I've missed you, too." The smile had vanished but Shelley couldn't help it.

Shelley took the shortcut back to Baker House, getting madder and madder with every step. Why didn't she agree to go out with Tom? So what if it was a last minute date? He wouldn't have asked her if he didn't want to be with her, would he? Maybe he really didn't have a date with Elizabeth this evening. Maybe she just imagined that Elizabeth had broken the date. After all, she did have an overactive imagination. At least that's what Dana always told her! Dana! This was all Dana's fault, Shelley suddenly decided. She would have agreed to go out with Tom if it wasn't for Dana. *The only reason I said no was just to please my roommate!*

Dana, totally unaware of the thoughts rioting in Shelley's head, just happened to be walking down the steps when Shelley barged into the entry hall.

"This is all your fault!" Shelley yelled.

Dana automatically looked behind her, to see if anyone else was standing behind her. "Are you yelling at me?" she asked.

"I certainly am," Shelley said. "Tom just asked me out for tonight and I told him no," Shelley said. She was good and miserable! Her eyes stung from trying not to cry, and her arms ached from clutching her books in a death grip.

"Shelley, what are you talking about? What is all my fault?"

"That I told Tom I couldn't go out with him tonight even though I really want to."

"Why did you do that?" Dana asked.

"Because of you! I knew you wouldn't accept a date at the last minute, but I would . . . except I didn't," she added with a groan.

"Shelley, you aren't making any sense. You're obviously upset. Now if you'll just calm down."

"I don't want to calm down," Shelley insisted. "I'm upset because of all the smiling I've had to do all week," she exaggerated. "And I'm through smiling, Dana. Got that?"

Dana didn't answer. Shelley ran up the steps, past Dana, sobbing with loud gasps and gulps that made Dana want to cringe.

"And I'm through with your stupid health diet, too," Shelley yelled over her shoulder.

Dana stood alone in the entry hall, wondering where she went wrong. "What did I do?" she asked the empty hall.

Faith explained it to Dana as she prepared for her date with Johnny. "Shelley says you're too bossy and she's tired of it. She says you're always finding faults with her."

"That's not true," Dana protested. She plopped down on her bed and then added, "You don't think that's true, do you Faith? Am I picking on Shelley?"

Faith heard the hint of sadness in Dana's voice. "No, I don't think you've been picking on her at all," she said. "The truth, as I see it, is that Shelley really wanted to go out with Tom but knew that she was his second choice so she didn't. It's easier to blame you since you've been trying to get her to cheer up."

"Now she's furious with *me*," Dana said. "Honestly, Faith, you try to help someone and what do you get? I called Maggie," Dana said next, changing the subject. "She's coming up next weekend. Who can we get to babysit her while we do our hospital duties?"

"Babysit? Dana, your sister isn't a baby."

"I know," Dana amended. "I just meant, who can we get to entertain her while we're at the hospital."

"I'll check around and you do the same. Maybe Mary Beth could keep her busy."

Just then Shelley came into the room. She took a deep breath before looking directly at Dana. "I'm sorry, Dana. I overreacted," she admitted. "I've just been so miserable lately and. . . ."

She started to cry, her shoulders slumped with despair and Dana didn't get mad this time. "I know you hate it when I cry," Shelley muttered as Faith handed her a Kleenex, "and I'm tired of it, too. It's just that. . . ."

"You can't help it, I know," Dana said, sighing.

Casey appeared at the doorway. "Hope I'm not interrupting but your date is here, Faith. Shelley, what's the matter?" she asked, hovering in the doorway.

"She's a little sad," Dana said, realizing that was probably the understatement of the year.

"Hey, Shelley. You should be happy. I heard what happened at play practice," she added.

"You heard about Tom asking me out?" Shelley said with a muffled sob.

Casey walked into the room and sat down beside Shelley. She draped her arm over Shelley's shoulders and said, "No, silly. I heard that Miss Perfect isn't so perfect."

"Oh, that," Shelley replied. "Well, we all have a bad day, I guess."

"Tell me what happened!" Faith demanded. Now she hovered in the doorway, her purse in her hands. "But hurry, Johnny's waiting."

Casey told the story about Elizabeth Kennedy's little scene during play practice, obviously relishing every detail.

"That's food for thought," Faith said before leaving.

"What did she mean by that?" Shelley asked Dana.

"Maybe that Elizabeth is human like the rest of us, Shelley," Dana said.

"Shelley, your cheeks are going to get chapped if you don't stop crying," Casey said. Shelley immediately quit crying and reached for her lotion.

"Come on," Casey said, grabbing Shelley's arm. "Let's hit the machines for a snack."

"Are you back on our diet?" Dana asked Shelley.

"I've got to have some chocolate, Dana," Shelley protested. "How about a little moderation?" she asked, her voice hopeful.

"Chocolate and moderation and you don't mix," Dana stated. She was smiling and Shelley didn't take offense.

"Well, I guess I'll get ready for my date with Keith then," Casey said and left.

"Here it is Friday night and neither of us have dates," Shelley said gloomily.

"Shelley," Dana said suddenly. "Terry and

Sheff are going to the Oakley-Greenleaf hockey game. Let's go with them."

"Don't they have dates?" Shelley asked.

"No," Dana explained. "Come on, don't even take time to think about it. We'll have fun. Johnny and Faith will be there, too."

Faith and Johnny had front row seats at the hockey game. Faith had her camera loaded and ready, thinking that the pictures would be nice for the *Clarion*. While they waited for the game to begin, Faith told Johnny about Shelley's latest trauma. She didn't feel she was betraying a confidence and knew that Johnny really cared about her roommates. "I don't understand," Johnny told Faith when she had finished with the story. "Shelley got upset because Tom asked her out?"

"Yes," Faith said.

"That doesn't make much sense," Johnny said.

"Sometimes Shelley doesn't make much sense," Faith grinned.

Sheff, Terry, Shelley, and Dana all yelled a greeting and invaded the front row. Dana quickly took Faith's camera and suggested that she get a picture of the two of them together. Johnny put his arm around Faith. "Great idea, Dana. I'd like a picture of the two of us."

More pictures followed, of the entire gang, until Faith had to call a halt. "I want to take some pictures of the game," she said. "For the *Clarion*."

"Hey, guess who's sitting behind us, about ten rows back," Dana whispered to Faith.

"Who?"

"Tom and Elizabeth, that's who," Dana said. "Should we tell Shelley?"

"Not while she's smiling. Let her have a good time," Faith said. "If you tell her, she'll just remember she's supposed to be upset."

Dana nodded, agreeing completely.

A short time later, Shelley nudged Dana. "Guess what!" She could barely contain her excitement.

"What?"

"Tom's here with Elizabeth!"

Dana blinked in amazement. Shelley seemed thrilled with her news, and that didn't make any sense at all. "And that makes you happy?"

"Of course," Shelley said, clasping her hands together. "That means he asked me out first, not second, and that Elizabeth didn't break her date with him when she whispered something to him on the stage." She paused for a breath, beaming, and then continued, "Unless of course, she did break the date and then changed her mind and called him. I hadn't thought of that," she stated. "But it doesn't matter, does it?"

"Shelley, you've lost me," Dana admitted. "But if you're happy, so be it."

"I'm happy. Dana, things are starting to look up."

Shelley decided later that she had spoken too soon. When the game was over Tom and

Elizabeth walked ahead of the group to the parking lot, and Shelley could easily see that Tom had his arm around his date. The happiness bubble popped, and Shelley grew silent and thoughtful. No one noticed, though, until they all descended on Pizza Pete's.

Dana looked over at Shelley, squeezed between Terry and Sheff on the other side of the booth and noticed she was looking past them, towards the door. Dana automatically turned, and immediately spotted Tom and Elizabeth as they walked through the door. They were holding hands and smiling.

Dana nudged Faith under the table, no easy task, since Johnny was sitting between them. When Faith glanced over, Dana motioned to the door with her eyes.

Everyone ignored the twosome from that point on. At first Faith tried to involve Shelley in conversation, but after five minutes of one word answers, she gave up. As long as Tom and Elizabeth were seated right across the room, nothing was going to cheer Shelley up.

Shelley thought she put up a pretty good front. She kept trying to smile even though she didn't participate in the conversation. And she never looked across the room the entire time they were there . . . at least no more than once or twice, she told herself.

Terry treated everyone to a large pizza with all Shelley's favorite trimmings but she hardly ate any. Dana noticed that the strain between Sheff and Johnny had ended. At one time Johnny had considered the sophisticated Sheff a real threat to his peace of mind, but now he realized that Faith didn't have any interest in Sheff as a boyfriend.

"Hey, there's Tom," Sheff said when the group got up to leave.

Shelley groaned and Faith heard her. "Come on. We're going over to that table and say hello," she announced.

"Are you serious?" Shelley whispered with barely suppressed outrage.

"Very."

They all circled the table containing Elizabeth and Tom, and Faith introduced everyone. "Did you go to the game?" she asked innocently.

"Sure did," Tom said. He was looking at Shelley as he spoke. Terry slid his arm protectively around Shelley's shoulder and smiled at Tom.

"Wasn't it exciting?" Elizabeth stated. She smiled at everyone until she focused on Shelley. Then she made her face a blank.

"Yes," Shelley heard herself answer for the group. "We better get going," she added when Elizabeth continued to ignore her.

"Better go home and study your lines in case something happens to the star," Elizabeth called after her.

So it was a snide remark, Shelley thought. She wished she could think of something to say in retaliation. Unfortunately, she couldn't. She just wasn't quick enough. It was difficult to be miserable and witty at the same time.

Chapter Twelve

Saturday turned out to be quite hectic. By the time Dana finished her four hours at the hospital, she was exhausted. Terry was, of course, the reason.

She only had half an hour to go and was really enjoying herself as she helped change and adjust diets. 311 was no longer on soft foods; 218 was back to high protein. Dana handled it all with ease, feeding the information into the computer the way she had been taught, and gaining approval and praise from her instructor. Then Terry arrived, a little breathless and flushed. "Dana, I need to see you for a few minutes," he said with a rush. "In the hall, okay?"

"I've only got a half hour to go," Dana said, checking her watch. "Can't it wait?"

"Dana, this is an emergency," Terry said, stressing every word.

The sound of his voice told Dana he was quite serious. She nodded, asked for permission to leave for a few minutes, and followed Terry outside the kitchen.

"It's bad," Terry warned her. "When this is over, I'm telling you, Dana, medicine and hospitals are out. I'm not cut out for this stuff," Terry said.

"What happened?" Dana asked.

"I feel awful," Terry began.

"What are the symptoms," she asked, trying to sound sympathetic.

"It's not me," Terry said, clearly frustrated. "I'm fine. I mean, I think I'm fine. Why? Do I look a little sick?"

"No, no," Dana said. "You don't look sick, you look upset."

"Well, darn it, I have a reason to look upset!" Terry acted like Dana was being critical.

She hurried to placate him, growing more confused by the second. "Terry what is the matter with you?"

"It's that nice Mr. Emery," Terry began. He couldn't look at Dana but kept his eyes downcast.

"Oh no," Dana said. "I remember him. He always has two breakfasts every Saturday," she added. "Oh, what happened to him. Did he take a turn for the worse?"

"Sort of," Terry said, not understanding where Dana's thoughts were leading.

"He just had foot surgery," Dana said, more to herself than to Terry. "Oh, poor Mr. Emery. Did he go quickly?"

"He sure did," Terry said. "One minute he was there, and the next —"

"Poor Terry! I hadn't realized you were so close to him. And I thought he was getting well."

"Dana, what are you talking about?" Terry suddenly seemed to come to attention, staring intently at Dana.

"Mr. Emery," Dana said. "I thought you said he —"

"I lost him!"

"He's here somewhere," Dana said. "I'll check out with the kitchen and help you," she added.

Terry sighed with relief. "I knew I could count on you," he said. "I'm going to start in the basement and work my way up. You take the top floor and work your way down. Okay?"

"Can we just ask the operator to page him?"

"Are you serious? Then everyone would know I lost him," Terry said, shocked at her suggestion.

Dana nodded. "We'll find him. I promise," Dana said, smiling.

And they did, almost twenty minutes later. Dana realized when she spotted him that she should have looked there first. Mr. Emery was treating himself to an early lunch in the hospital cafeteria.

She sat with him while he finished his meal and then wheeled him down to X-ray. And then she went looking for Terry. She found him up on the pediatrics floor, pouring his heart and his story out to Shelley.

"Mr. Emery is down in X-ray," Dana told Terry. "I found him in the cafeteria."

Terry reacted just like a bottle of soda pop that had been shaken and then opened. He exploded with his thanks and gratitude. "I really owe you," he repeated again and again. He started down the hall, whistling, and then called over his shoulder, "And Dana? If you tell a soul what happened, I'll throttle you."

Dana grinned. She turned back to Shelley and said, "Let's look for Faith."

Dana found Faith in the Emergency Room, talking with Dr. Webster. Dana hated to intrude, but they both saw her when she peeked around the corner so she had to continue on into the area. "Are you ready to leave?"

"Yes," Faith said. "I'll see you later, Frank," she told the doctor.

"About seven?" Frank suggested.

"That would be fine," Faith said.

She followed Dana out of the building after they had each collected their things, and waited patiently for Dana to ask the questions she was sure her roommate had.

"So what's happening?" Dana finally asked, trying to sound very nonchalant.

"What do you mean?" Faith asked, wide eyed.

"Don't be coy with me," Dana demanded. "So tell me before Shelley and Terry get here. What's this about seven tonight?"

"Frank is taking me out to dinner," Faith said.

"You've got a date with him," Dana said, sounding excited.

"I'm not sure if it's a date or not," Faith admitted. "I took some pictures of him and he's paying me back by taking me out for dinner."

"Why did he want pictures of himself?" Dana asked.

"His parents wanted him to send them some," Faith explained. "So tell me, Dana, is it a date or what?" She tried to sound neutral about the question but inside she was really nervous. Did she want it to be a real date or not?

"It's a date, I think," Dana said. "At least I'd call it a date. Wouldn't you?"

"Yeah, I guess so," Faith said, smiling. "He's really very nice, don't you think?"

"Yes," Dana said.

Terry and Shelley appeared, only to announce that they were going to stay in town for the afternoon and do some shopping. Dana and Faith decided not to join them and walked back to Canby Hall.

CHAPTER THIRTEEN

That evening Faith was in the Baker Hall lobby pacing the floor. Frank was fifteen minutes late for their date and those minutes were sheer agony for Faith. Maybe there was an emergency at the hospital and he couldn't leave, Faith considered. Or maybe he'd forgotten all about their date, she thought. She chewed on her lower lip while she considered that possibility, decided she would give him another fifteen minutes, and then call.

Faith looked at herself in the octagon shaped mirror as she smoothed her dress. She looked very grown up, she decided. Sheff suddenly appeared beside her in the mirror and gave her a slow, exaggerated wink. Then he stepped back, looked her up and down very slowly, and whistled. He never said a word, but he didn't need to. His appreciative eyes said it all. Faith smiled, hoping inside that Frank would react the same way. Of course, she warned herself, he was several years older than Sheff and was probably used to going out with women. Faith knew she was attractive, but didn't consider that of much significance. It was what was inside that was important. That's what her mother had often said, and Faith knew she was right.

Frank Webster walked into the entry hall at that moment. "Hi there," he greeted her with a smile. "Faith, you look sensational."

Faith smiled, thought from the way he was inspecting her that he really meant the compliment, and said, "Hello, yourself. You look sensational, too. Here are your pictures, Frank. Would you like to go through them now?"

"Better wait until we're at the restaurant," Frank answered. "I got lost and accidentally went to the wrong dorm," he explained. "Our reservations are in fifteen minutes so we better hustle."

Faith nodded and reached for her coat. Frank quickly took it from her and helped her put it on. Then he put his hand on her shoulder and opened the door for her. Faith felt her heart beat a little faster.

She wasn't sure where she should sit in the car, how close, and finally settled on leaning against the door and turning so that she could face him.

"Don't forget your seatbelt," Frank said as he buckled his on.

"Johnny always reminds me about that too," Faith said.

"Who's Johnny?" Frank asked.

"My boyfriend," Faith answered. "He lives in Greenleaf."

"Tell me about him," Frank suggested.

"He's very nice," Faith said. "He wants to be a detective and that was a real problem for me in the beginning, and, well, it still is sometimes."

"Why is it a problem?" Frank asked, casting her a glance.

"My father was a policeman and he was killed. I guess I'm afraid to care about anyone in that line of work."

They pulled to a stop at a traffic light and Frank turned his full attention to Faith. "That must have been tough on you, Faith. That's probably the reason you're so controlled."

Faith raised her eyebrows. "Controlled?"

"I bet you keep things inside most of the time," Frank said. "You control your reactions, your emotions. At least that's how you seem to me."

The light changed and Frank returned his concentration to driving. Faith was glad. She didn't want him to see how his words had affected her. He was so astute, so in tune with how she felt inside. Johnny was, too, she reminded herself. But it had taken him longer to understand her, much longer.

"I guess you're right. It's difficult for me to say what I'm feeling," she admitted.

"That can be good and bad," Frank said. "I'm pretty much the same way though. Guess

we're both just private people," he chuckled.
"Hey! Let's do a radical change for tonight."

"What?" Faith smiled at the eagerness in
his voice. "What do you have in mind?"

"Let's make a pact. We'll be completely
honest and open to each other, tell each
other what we're thinking, okay?"

Faith didn't immediately answer. "It might
turn out to be embarrassing," she warned.

"We can handle that," Frank assured her.
He was in the process of parking the car
between two others on one of the side streets
of Greenleaf. "Well, what do you say?"

"Okay." She was committed, and found
herself looking forward to the change. "No
matter what, I'll tell you what I'm thinking,
and you have to do the same."

"You got it." Frank started laughing and
Faith joined in.

"What is so funny?" she asked as he helped
her out of the car.

"I'm just having a good time," he told her.
"You're going to love this place," he continued. "I happened on it a couple of weeks
ago and it's the best kept secret in Greenleaf."

There wasn't even a sign on the door, Faith
noticed, as she walked inside. The restaurant
was lovely with candles lit on each table. It
was a warm, cozy place and very crowded.
"The best kept secret is out by the looks of
the crowd," Faith said.

Frank gave his name to the owner and they
were immediately shown to a table towards
the back of the restaurant. It was a bit more

secluded and Faith was secretly pleased.

Frank ordered for both of them and Faith went along, until she found out one of the dishes consisted of squid. "You can have all of that," she told Frank.

"Be daring," Frank suggested.

"I don't want to," Faith said, then she smiled. "I'm being open and honest, remember?"

Frank laughed and reached for the folder Faith had carried in. "Let's have a look," he suggested.

"I hope you like them," Faith said, trying to hold her breath.

"If I don't, I'll have to tell you," Frank said with a smile.

"Hey, that's right," Faith said. She watched nervously as Frank looked inside the folder.

"I love them!" he exclaimed. Faith knew he was being honest. "My folks are going to be so pleased," he said. "You're really something, Faith, very talented."

"Thank you."

"Hey, I mean it. You know you're talented, don't you?"

This honesty thing was starting to be a little difficult. Faith said as much. "Frank, if I tell you I think I am talented, then you'll think I'm conceited, and if I tell you I don't think I'm talented, you'll think I'm being humble but I'll really be lying."

"I'll tell you exactly how I'm feeling. I have to, remember?" Frank said.

"Then yes, I think I am talented. Photography is my passion and my future, I hope. I want to be the best."

"You will be," Frank said. "You're good enough. In my humble opinion anyway," Frank said.

"I'm glad you think so," Faith said very seriously.

"Is it important what I think about you?" Frank asked.

"Yes."

"That's nice," Frank said. "If I had a little sister, I'd want her to be you."

Faith frowned. Before she could lose her courage, she said, "I don't want to be your sister. I'd rather be your girlfriend."

Frank didn't immediately react. Faith wished she could disappear, she felt so embarrassed. She looked down at her hands, berating herself for being honest. She finally took the courage to look up at Frank, trying to think of something to say in order to change the subject. What she saw in his eyes stopped all her thoughts. There was gentleness and caring there, and something else.

"You're entirely too young for me, Faith," Frank told her. He was using his serious voice, but his eyes were sparkling. "But in ten years, when we're both rich and famous and ready to settle down, I hope you'll think about me and maybe look me up. You're a special person, very, very special."

Faith smiled. "In ten years you'll probably be married and have five kids," she predicted.

Frank shook his head. "Nope. I have to

graduate from medical school this spring, do a year's internship, a three year surgical residency, and then set up a practice somewhere."

"Good heavens, I'll be established and world famous before you," Faith said, laughing.

"When your picture is on the cover of *Newsweek*, will you still remember me?" Frank teased back.

"I'll try," Faith told him. "Why did you decide to be a surgeon?" she asked.

Frank immediately launched into his reasons, and continued to talk all through dinner. He cajoled Faith into trying one bite of his squid, and Faith did her best not to gag.

He made Faith sign her name on the back of the photographs, with her home address for future references, he said, and Faith was happy to oblige. "Someday this picture could be famous because it's the first one you signed."

"I think you believe in me more than I do," Faith told him.

They went for a ride after dinner and Frank showed her the house he and two other soon-to-be doctors rented rooms in. Then they drove around the little town of Greenleaf and Frank spotted the Tutti-Frutti. "I could use some ice cream," he announced.

Faith agreed, not wanting the evening to end so soon. They walked inside and ended up sitting in Johnny and Faith's favorite booth.

Faith ordered a single dip of vanilla ice

cream, in case she accidentally spilled on her white dress, and Frank ordered a strawberry soda.

They were talking quietly when Faith glanced up and saw Johnny standing in the doorway. He had such a surprised and hurt look on his face that Faith was momentarily frozen in place. Then Johnny turned and walked back out the door. That got Faith moving. "I'll be right back," she told Frank as she bolted out of the booth. She ran to the front and out the door, but Johnny was nowhere to be seen.

She called his name twice and then gave up and slowly walked back inside the ice cream shop. "I thought I saw someone I know," she told Frank, "and I wanted to introduce you."

A rather loud argument, coming from across the room, drew both Frank's and Faith's attention. The cause was Elizabeth Kennedy. "That girl sure does have a temper," Frank said in a conspiratorial whisper. "Look at the guy she's with, he's turning three shades of red. Bet his blood pressure is way up."

Faith had to laugh at his medical evaluation. "I know that blood pressure case and he deserves a few heart palpitations," Faith said. "He dumped my roommate," Faith confided.

"Then I won't rush over and take his pulse," Frank teased.

"Hey, Dr. Webster, how you doing?" Terry's voice was full of cheer. Faith didn't even look up. She just moved over in the booth so that Terry could join them. "Boy, am I glad I ran into you," he said.

"Need another consult?" Frank asked good-naturedly.

"Well, I was wondering about something," Terry began. He suddenly seemed to notice Faith for the first time, though she had been staring at him ever since he invaded the booth. "Hi, Faith. Gee, you look nice." He turned back to Frank and asked, "Can a guy develop flat feet overnight? My arches seem to be falling."

Frank was sensitive and didn't even smile. Faith couldn't help herself. She burst out laughing.

"Let me see your shoes," Frank said. That statement made Faith laugh all the louder.

"What's so funny?" Both Terry and Frank looked puzzled.

"I thought you were going to ask him to let you look at his feet," Faith told them, vastly amused.

Frank continued to look puzzled. "I was," he admitted.

At Faith's startled expression, Frank started to laugh. "I'm only teasing."

Terry was standing up, staring at his rather desperate-looking tennis shoes.

Frank looked down at Terry's shoes and shook his head. "Those should have been retired a year ago. Buy a new pair and your arches will feel better," he predicted.

Terry was relieved. "Think that's all it is?" he asked, sitting down again. Before Frank could answer, he launched into a few more symptoms he was having, and Faith's thoughts turned to Johnny. She would have to call him in the morning, she decided, just to set him straight. Part of her rebelled at that idea. He never even gave her the opportunity to explain. He just walked away.

Talk about convicting on circumstantial evidence! Some detective he was going to make! Faith realized she was fuming, and promptly stopped herself. Why, she was acting just like Shelley, she suddenly realized! Shelley had blamed Dana when she turned Tom down for a date. *Now I'm blaming Johnny and this is my fault.*

Terry stood up and Faith tried to concentrate on what he was saying. He was telling Frank he was meeting some people and that made Faith glance around again. Johnny! He was back, hovering in the doorway, staring at her. Faith's whole body reacted. She was smiling from head to toe! "Excuse me a minute," she said to Frank and Terry. With slow, measured steps, she walked over to Johnny. When she reached him, she took hold of his hand and started to drag him back to the booth. "I don't want to interrupt," he said in a quiet, very controlled voice.

"You're not interrupting. Come on. I want you to meet someone." Faith ignored his resistance and pulled him along. When they reached the booth she didn't let go of his hand. "Now then," Faith said with a smile.

"Dr. Webster, I'd like you to meet my boy-friend, Johnny."

She turned to Johnny and said, "And this is Dr. Frank Webster, Johnny. Shake hands and say hello."

Johnny remembered his manners, pulled free of Faith's hand and extended it to Frank. "Faith has told me all about you," Frank said, shaking Johnny's hand.

Johnny seemed real surprised by that statement and grinned. "Hope it was all good," he replied. "How did you two meet?"

"At the hospital," Faith supplied. Terry filled Johnny in on the rest of the story, about Faith taking pictures for Frank's father and mother and how Frank was paying her back with a free dinner.

"I've got to go," Terry advised when he finished telling Johnny about Frank.

"So it wasn't a date," Johnny whispered in Faith's ear. Frank heard and shook his head.

"Not this time, but I give you fair warning, Johnny. In ten years I'm coming back and give you a run for your money. It's every man for himself then," he said.

Faith knew Frank was just being nice but she felt very special. She laughed and took hold of Johnny's hand again. "He made me try squid," she told him, changing the subject.

Johnny stayed a few more minutes and then he stood and gave Faith's hand a little squeeze. "I've got to go. I'll call you tomor-row," he said.

Faith was very quiet on the ride back to Baker House with Frank. Frank finally broke the silence. "Do you think you might have a little crush on me?" he asked.

"I think I might," Faith answered.

"That's nice," Frank said. He took hold of her hand, patted it, and then let go. Little nerve endings went absolutely crazy and Faith's hand started to tingle. No doubt about it, she told herself, it was a crush all right!

She sighed, confused. "What's the matter?" Frank asked.

"I'm fickle," Faith said. "I've got a crush on you and I'm in love with Johnny. And that's fickle."

Frank laughed. "There's nothing wrong with caring for two people. One's going to be out of the picture next Wednesday though. I'm leaving."

"Oh." Faith felt like a balloon with all the air let out. Totally deflated.

"My rotation is over," Frank explained.

Frank walked her to the front door and told her how much he had enjoyed their evening. Then he leaned down and gave her a soft kiss on the forehead. It was like a big brother sort of kiss, but Faith didn't mind. "Remember," he teased when he let go of her shoulders. "Ten years. Okay?"

Faith nodded. "Thank you, Frank," she said. "For everything."

She wasn't referring to the lovely evening, he realized. She was thanking him for being such a gentle, understanding man. He was the first older man that Faith had ever had a crush on, and he hadn't laughed or made it a painful experience for her. He had made it wonderful! And she would never, ever forget him, she told herself.

Faith was sound asleep when Dana and Shelley stumbled into the room. The two girls quietly got ready for bed. Shelley didn't go through the lotion ritual. She was too tired. Dana was wondering if Faith had had a good time and glanced over at the sleeping form. Her question was answered. Faith was smiling in her sleep.

CHAPTER FOURTEEN

Patrice Allardyce walked to the center of the stage in the auditorium and clapped her hands for silence. The dignified headmistress of Canby Hall was wearing a wool blue suit and a cream colored blouse. Her hair was pulled back into its usual twist and every hair was in place.

The auditorium was packed, as the assembly was required, and only a note from the nurse stating that the student was terminally indisposed could get a student out of attending.

The headmistress went through the business of the week and then asked, "Would the three girls modeling the uniforms please join me on the stage?"

Everyone looked around, looking for the three girls. Dana sat between Shelley and Faith and listened to the escalating whispers and snickers. "Where's Pamela?" she finally asked.

Faith giggled. "There she comes," she said. "Late as usual."

"She looks like she just got out of bed," Shelley stated.

They watched as Pamela hurried to join the other girls on the stage. She was trying to tuck in the blouse to her uniform and act nonchalant at the same time.

Miss Allardyce waited until Pamela was finished tucking and straightening and then turned back to the audience. "Each of the girls will now parade across the stage. Pamela, you begin."

Pamela didn't seem overly pleased with the request. She sort of stomped across the stage, her arms folded across her chest. "Something tells me Pamela's heart just isn't in this," Casey whispered from behind the three roommates.

Pamela finished her stroll and stood to one side, glaring at the audience. The other two models were more enthusiastic in showing off their uniforms. Mary Beth had the most fun. She glided across the stage just like she was wearing a pair of ice skates. Her hands were on her hips, and her head tilted back in a dramatic gesture. The entire student body broke out in laughter, and there were whistles of appreciation and lots of clapping.

Patrice Allardyce wasn't amused. Her special glare stopped the noise immediately.

"How does she do that?" Shelley asked. "If I could imitate her gestures I'd be a famous actress," she told Faith.

"Takes years and years of practice," Faith decided.

"This is all so stupid," Casey muttered. The girls were sitting in the third row, and the headmistress, from the look on her face, had heard the remark.

"Casey Flint, did you have a comment you wished to share with the assembly?" she asked.

The three roommates all gasped and promptly slid lower in their seats, trying to disappear. "Casey, hurry up and apologize," Dana whispered over her shoulder.

"Dana Morrison? Did you have a remark you wished to make?"

Dana felt herself turning beet red. She started to stand up, intending to apologize, but felt Casey's hands settle on her shoulders, holding her down.

Then Casey jumped to her feet, cleared her throat, and called out, "I was just remarking on the uniform, Ms. Allardyce."

"And what was the remark?" the headmistress asked, her voice neutral.

The auditorium was so quiet that Shelley suddenly knew what people meant when they said it was so quiet you could hear a pin drop. She didn't think anyone was even breathing.

"I was . . . uh, I was commenting on the fact that I thought the uniforms were kind of stupid," she said.

Dana gasped again and then jumped to her feet. "She means that they're a little silly," she interjected.

"Ms. Allardyce, I think we should vote

now on the uniforms instead of waiting another two weeks," Casey called out. She
looked around the room and smiled when she
saw lots of students nodding their agreement.

"She means that everyone has had enough
time to make up their minds," Dana interjected.

The neutral expression finally left Patrice
Allardyce's face. "Miss Morrison," the headmistress said, "Casey and I both speak Eng-
lish. We do not need an interpreter. Kindly
sit down."

"You are of the opinion that we should
vote now?" Ms. Allardyce asked Casey.

"Yes," Casey called out. Dana could hear
the nervousness in Casey's voice and then
felt Casey tugging on her hair. She tried to
pull her head free of Casey's grasp but finally
gave up. She could stand a little pain if it
helped Casey's nerves.

"Since it was decided that the uniform issue
would be handled in a democratic fashion,
all those in favor of voting now instead of
waiting for another two weeks, please stand
up."

The auditorium exploded into action.
Everyone stood up. Everyone, that is, except
Dana. Casey's death grip on her hair disal-
lowed much movement. When Casey finally
realized what she was doing, and let go of
Dana, then Dana joined the rest of the as-
sembly. "Looks pretty unanimous to me,"
Shelley said with a grin.

"Majority rules," Ms. Allardyce said.

"Everyone please sit down. Miss Flint, since it was your suggestion that the vote take place now, you will now come forward and take over."

Casey nodded, tripped over books and feet, and made her way to the stage. "Everyone take a piece of paper from their notebook and vote yes or no. If it's okay, we'll count them right now. Okay, Ms. Allardyce?" she asked.

The headmistress nodded and Dana thought she saw a hint of a smile at the corners of the headmistress' mouth.

Bedlam ruled for the next five minutes while everyone voted. Those seated at the ends of the row counted up their votes and then gave them to Casey.

The uniforms were clearly defeated. When Casey made the announcement, the auditorium exploded into cheers of delight. Even Pamela smiled.

Friday night all the girls were waiting for Maggie to arrive. Faith was already dressed in her white wool dress. She explained that Johnny wanted to take her someplace special.

"I think he's trying to compete with Frank," Dana said.

Faith nodded. She had already figured that out. "It's totally unnecessary. Frank and Johnny are as different as night and day. Besides, Frank left Greenleaf Wednesday. He's at Boston General now."

There was a timid knock on the door and

Dana answered it. Maggie stood in the door-way, carrying enough luggage to last her a month. "Are you moving in?" Dana teased.

"I'm like a girl scout," Maggie said with a sheepish grin. "I'm always prepared."

Dana hugged her little sister and pulled her into the room. She quickly introduced her to the roommates.

"You got all dressed up for me?" Maggie teased Faith.

"Sorry to disappoint you," Faith told her, "But I have a special date. I'll tell you all about it later," she promised as she hurried out of the room.

"Maggie? How would you like a semi-date tonight?" Dana asked her sister.

"What's a semi-date?" she asked.

"That's when you go out with a boy, but Dana and I tag along," Shelley explained. "Terry is going to take you to a soccer game and we want to come along."

"Am I dressed all right or should I change?" she asked. Maggie was wearing a pair of designer jeans and a checked blouse. Dana took a good look at her and realized how grown up she looked. She was, Dana decided, blossoming.

"You look wonderful," she told her sister. "And I like your hair. You got it cut, didn't you?"

"Last week," Maggie said. Dana decided not to talk to Maggie about Canby Hall until the next day, when she returned from the hospital.

"And tomorrow Mary Beth is going to show you around the place while Dana and Faith and I are in town doing our hospital work," she heard Shelley explain to her sister. "You're going to sleep in Casey's room. Come on and I'll help you unpack before your big date."

The rest of the evening was filled with fun and laughter. Terry teased and joked until Maggie said that her face hurt from smiling so much.

When Maggie, Shelley, and Dana returned to 407, Faith was back from her date. "We went to a wonderful restaurant and it was very romantic. You know, it was fun getting all dressed up and we promised to do it more often," Faith continued. "But tomorrow we're going to the mixer in jeans."

"Hey, what am I going to wear to the mixer?" Shelley asked. "Tom will probably be there with Elizabeth and I want to look super."

"Hey, that reminds me," Faith suddenly remembered. "I saw Tom and Elizabeth at the Tutti-Frutti last Friday night. I forgot all about it," she said to Shelley.

"I don't want to hear," Shelley muttered.

"No, listen. Elizabeth was. . . ."

"Don't say another word. It will just depress me," Shelley said.

"Tell me," Dana insisted with a yawn. "I want to hear."

"It was quite a scene," Faith said. "Elizabeth was yelling at Tom about something and he looked like he wanted to crawl into the nearest hole."

"He did?" Shelley asked, her eyes wide with delight.

"I thought you didn't want to hear," Faith said.

"Well, that certainly explains it," Shelley said.

"Explains what?" Maggie asked.

"Tom has been real quiet at play practice all week. He sits by himself whenever he isn't on stage. And I've been trying to ignore him, too" she added. "Poor Tom! He must be miserable." The smile she wore contradicted her words.

"*Poor* Tom has it coming. Are you going to dance with him tomorrow night?" Dana asked.

"Yes, I am," Shelley said. "If he asks me, I will."

Dana didn't get the opportunity to have a long, serious talk with Maggie until Sunday morning. After breakfast, Dana insisted on taking Maggie for a long walk. They were finally alone, strolling along the path that led to the headmistress' house, when Dana got up the nerve to talk about Canby Hall.

"Mom says you'll probably come up here next year," she began. "I have to tell you, Maggie, that I have mixed feelings about it. I'm not trying to hurt your feelings or anything," she rushed to add, "but. . . ."

"You have mixed feelings!" Maggie seemed

amazed. "I'm the one with the mixed feelings, Dana," she said. She frowned, took a deep breath, and then said, "Look, I don't want to hurt your feelings either, but we better come to some decisions, or. . . ."

"What are you talking about?" Dana asked, clearly puzzled.

"Oh Dana, I've kept rehearsing how I would tell you what I'm thinking but I've forgotten my lines," she said.

Dana smiled, realizing she had done the same thing, and said, "Just tell me what's going on in that head of yours."

"Okay, big sister, it's like this. I think I'd like to transfer up here but you're the main reason I'm still undecided. I've got to level with you, Dana. Since you've been gone from home, I haven't been the little sister. Mom talks to me like an adult now, not the baby, and I like that. When you come home, everything reverts back to the way it was when I was a little kid. I don't make any decisions without talking to you. You're . . . kind of bossy."

Dana had to sit down. She couldn't believe what she was hearing. She pulled Maggie over to a bench and suggested they sit. Maggie shook her head, and started to pace back and forth in front of the bench where Dana sat. Dana watched her and listened. "If I come up here, I don't want to have to answer to you all the time. I don't want you to take care of me, Dana. I know I'm probably hurting you by saying that, but I want to be on my own. You know, make my own friends, my own mistakes. It's the only way I'll learn. My biggest worry is that you'll be looking over my shoulder all the time. There, I said it. Are you very angry?"

"Let me get this straight," Dana replied. "You're worried about me telling you what to do all the time?" she asked.

"Yes! Are you mad?" Maggie stopped right in front of Dana, put her hands on her hips, and waited for an answer.

Dana started to laugh. She couldn't help it. Relief did that to her, she thought. She felt the knot untie in her stomach, and completely disappear. It was all going to be okay.

"Maggie," Dana said. "I've been working myself up into a real anxiety attack over this, too," she sighed. "I thought you'd come up here and I'd have to play the big sister role all the time. You know, take care of you, fight your battles for you. . . ."

"That's what I don't want," Maggie protested. "Dana, we are both individuals besides sisters," she added.

"And I was worried I'd lose my new found independence," Dana admitted.

"I don't want to lose mine either."

Then they both started to laugh again. "Look, let's agree. If you come up here, you're on your own. If you want some big sister advice, you'll have to ask, okay? I won't interfere and try to run your life. I promise."

"Really? You might not be able to help yourself," Maggie told her. "You've been a big sister for a long time."

"I'll be there for you when you need me," Dana said. She turned serious. "I'll always be there for you, but I won't interfere."

"And I'll always be there for you, too," Maggie promised. She smiled. "I'm still not sure what I want to do, but I sure feel better about Canby now. Thanks for understanding."

Dana stood up and linked arms with Maggie. They started to walk back to Baker. Each was thinking her own thoughts. Dana couldn't believe the torment she had put herself through. She had to remember to thank Alison for suggesting that Maggie come up for a visit. She started to laugh again. The thought of a little junk food suddenly sounded very appealing. "Come on, Maggie. I'll treat you to a candy bar before you have to leave."

CHAPTER FIFTEEN

The roommates were in high spirits as they walked over to the auditorium the opening night of the spring play. "At least I don't have to go through the jitters tonight," Shelley said.

"Now *that's* thinking positive," Dana said.

When they entered the auditorium, Faith and Shelley went backstage, Faith to take pictures of the performance for the *Clarion*, and Shelley to wish everyone luck. Dana was saving her a place in the middle of the theater.

"Thank goodness you're here," Tom called when he spotted Shelley. He grabbed hold of her shoulders and gave her a tight squeeze.

"Why is that?" Shelley asked, continuing to smile.

"Elizabeth won't go on. She's crying like a baby and absolutely refuses. Hurry and get ready, Shelley. You've only got fifteen minutes before the curtain goes up."

"But . . . but. . . ."

"Shelley, get hold of yourself," Faith said, giving her a gentle nudge that dislodged her from Tom's hold. "You look a little sick."

"Faith, may I see you *alone* for a minute?" Shelley asked. "Will you excuse us, Tom?" she asked.

Shelley grabbed Faith by the arm and propelled her into a corner. "What am I going to do? Oh heavens, Faith, what am I going to do!"

"Get ready," Faith said firmly. "Right *now*!"

"You don't understand. . . ." Shelley began. "I . . . I. . . ." Shelley looked like she was about to cry.

Suddenly Shelley stopped herself, took a deep breath, and quit ringing her hands. Faith observed the quick change in her friend and blinked. Fire was there, in Shelley's eyes, and she looked like she was about to murder someone. "Come with me," she snapped at Faith. "You are about to witness the best performance of my life."

"What're you going to do?" Faith asked, frowning.

"I'm going to talk Elizabeth into going on. That, or kill her."

Faith meekly followed Shelley, thinking her roommate looked like a brooding tornado. Elizabeth was in the makeup room, crying her eyes out.

"I've had it with you, Elizabeth," Shelley

began. "Now get this, and get it good. You're going on, like it or not. You've had your little tantrum and that's okay. We'll just chalk it up to a case of stagefright. But it's time to grow up and quit acting like a baby. You're a wonderful actress and I know you're just a freshman. Heaven only knows you can't expect miracles from freshman, but you can give it a good try."

Elizabeth, Faith thought, looked quite stunned. She didn't think the freshman had ever been yelled at quite the way Shelley was yelling. Why, she almost looked a little afraid of Shelley.

"I'm scared," the girl wailed.

"Tough! That's normal," Shelley said. "Now wipe off your face and blow your nose. And quit crying. It's disgusting! Blubbering can ruin your voice."

She then pulled Elizabeth out of the chair she was huddling in and patted her on the back. "You'll do just fine. Now get going and break a leg."

"Break a leg?" Elizabeth sniffled. She looked completely bewildered.

"That's what you say in show business for good luck," Shelley explained. She smiled. "And if you don't get out there on that stage, I'll break *both* your legs."

Elizabeth smiled a little. She thought Shelley was teasing. Faith wasn't so sure.

Faith and Shelley stood together and watched the first act from the side of the stage. Elizabeth had recovered from her case of nerves and was doing a wonderful job. Shelley sighed with relief.

Later that night all three girls were sprawled across their mattresses in Room 407.

"I got a postcard from Dr. Webster," Faith said.

"Why didn't you tell us?" Dana demanded.

"It only came today and there wasn't time to show it to you. It was really sweet."

"So you don't miss him?" Dana asked.

"No," Faith said. "Well, maybe just a little. It was exciting and fun to have him pay attention to me. And now Johnny and I appreciate each other a little more, I think."

Shelley listened and smiled. She was so content inside and was frankly amazed and very pleased with herself. She had weathered a difficult time and made it without any battle scars. She had decided that she would go out with Tom if he asked her. In her heart she knew that he would. Why, he had stared at her all last week, during every play practice. But he was right, she told herself. Both of them needed to date other people, too.

Shelley looked up when she heard Dana say, "Well, I have to hand it to Elizabeth. She gave a wonderful performance."

"Not as good as the one I gave," Shelley said and then began giggling mischievously.

Dana looked at Faith. "What's she talking about?"

"Elizabeth had a huge case of stage fright," Faith began, "and Shelley gave her a fantastic pep talk and convinced her to go on." At this Shelley's giggles rang out even more loudly and she rolled onto her back.

Faith shrugged her shoulders at Dana's puzzled expression and continued. "You should have seen our Shelley. What a trooper! I knew how much she wanted to go on instead of Elizabeth, but she just did what she knew in her heart was the right thing."

"I'm really proud of you, Shelley," Dana said, with admiration in her eyes.

"Stop! Stop, you two!" Shelley shouted as she tried to control her laughter. "Wait 'til you hear the real reason why I talked Elizabeth into going on."

"The real reason?" Faith repeated blankly.

"I hadn't memorized the lines!" Shelley shouted just before her giggles overtook her again. "I didn't know *one word* of the play."

"Oh, Shel, how could you?" Dana exclaimed. She tried to look sternly at Shelley but a smile twisted at the corner of her cheek.

"Well, I'm proud of you, Shelley," Faith said. "You handled it with . . . style," she managed to say before she and Dana joined Shelley's laughter.

"That's one thing you can say about the girls in Room 407 — they have style!" Dana said.

"In one form or another," Shelley answered.